ENTER JIMMY STRANGE

'What type of skulduggery is the Master Mind contemplating this time?' That was the question put to Jimmy Strange by his long-suffering girlfriend Sandra. But the answer always depended on which type of criminals Jimmy was pitting his wits against. Whether they were poisoners, gunmen, murderers, drug dealers, or jewel thieves, they were all operating, untouched, outside the law — until Jimmy entered the scene — and he was not averse to using their own methods against them . . .

ERNEST DUDLEY

ENTER JIMMY STRANGE

Complete and Unabridged

LINFORD
Leicester

First published in Great Britain

First Linford Edition
published 2011

British Library CIP Data

Dudley, Ernest.
    Enter Jimmy Strange.- -
    (Linford mystery library)
    1. Strange, Jimmy (Fictitious character)- -
    Fiction. 2. Detective and mystery stories.
    3. Large type books.
    I. Title II. Series
    823.9′14–dc22

    ISBN 978–1–44480–570–3

Published by
F. A. Thorpe (Publishing)
Anstey, Leicestershire

Set by Words & Graphics Ltd.
Anstey, Leicestershire
Printed and bound in Great Britain by
T. J. International Ltd., Padstow, Cornwall

This book is printed on acid-free paper

1

The Fat Man

It began with a bump outside the Regis Hotel, that enormous and somewhat elaborately architectured edifice which domineeringly overlooks the Green Park in Piccadilly.

The day was warm and sunny, with a light breeze that fluttered the trees all the way down from Knightsbridge and went airily on until it lost itself somewhere in the eddies of petrol fumes, mechanical cacophony of the traffic and bitterly colourful profanity of taxi-drivers swirling round Piccadilly Circus.

Jimmy and Sandra had strolled through the Park, enjoying the sunshine that brightened the greenness of the trees and foliage and experiencing that certain zip in the air, which is London's own individual characteristic, no other city

1

knows. Their conversation was light-heartedly inconsequent, and a glance at his watch told Jimmy they had timed the end of their sauntering to coincide neatly with a pleasurably anticipatory sensation in the region of the larynx and the immediate proximity of the Regis Hotel American Bar.

With the prospect of pre-lunch *apéritif* bringing a decided lightness to his step, Jimmy, with Sandra on his arm, crossed over to the hotel and was about to urge her towards the great swing doors when a man, turning quickly from the taxi he had just paid off, cannoned into them. Fortunately for Sandra, Jimmy was between her and the man, his lean frame warding off the other, who was a large rotund individual. In fact it was the latter's stomach, that region of his anatomy being expansive and vulnerable, which took the full blame of the impact. Its owner emitted a cry of not inconsiderable distress, and rocking backwards on his feet, clasped expensively gloved hands over his injured protuberance, opening and shutting his mouth, fish-like, as he tried to regain his breath, all this to the accompaniment of a sustained rumbling groan.

Sandra moved towards him with impulsive sympathy. 'Are you all right?' she asked anxiously.

The man could only gasp and nod his head affirmatively, still unable to produce any words. Jimmy had grasped his arm to steady him, and was now patting his thick shoulder sympathetically. 'Sorry I happened to be in the way,' he said.

'My — my fault — ' the corpulent individual managed to wheeze. 'My fault — entirely.' He began to move towards the hotel entrance, Jimmy still keeping a firm hand on his arm.

'I should park yourself for a minute,' he suggested.

'No — no.' The other contrived to force a wan smile. 'I'm all right, thanks.'

By now, the commissionaire, witnessing the incident, had come forward solicitously, and with him lending a hand, the trio moved into the hotel vestibule, Sandra following.

'What about a spot of — er — tonic to

help pull yourself together?' Jimmy asked, as they paused on the other side of the swing doors.

The fat man's face brightened at the suggestion. 'Couldn't think of a better idea,' he said.

He was obviously very much recovered from the effects of the collision, his breathing was less stertorous and his plump features were regaining their colour. The commissionaire pocketed the generous tip that was placed in his waiting palm and withdrew. Jimmy, with regard for the other's corpulence and present incapacitated state, indicated the lifts that bore seekers after prospective libations down to the lower ground floor where the American Bar was located. The man's progress was rather more active now, though he still continued, gently, to massage his stomach with one hand, as Jimmy and Sandra accompanied him towards the down lift.

'American Bar.'

'Yessir.'

The lift-doors slid together with a sibilant murmur and down they went.

They found a quiet corner in the crowded bar and, while the large man relaxed with a sigh of contentment in a luxurious plush chair and Sandra made some bright small-talk, Jimmy attended to the important business of procuring the drinks. The white-coated waiter returned promptly with his order and placed the drinks on the table before them. Gin-and-orange for Sandra and a Scotch for Jimmy and the other.

Followed the usual necessary pause in the conversation. Then, his chubby face pink and shining and his eyes bright, the big man lowered his glass to observe:

'Just what the doctor ordered, eh?'

Jimmy grinned at him in agreement. He said:

'Makes the world look brighter all right.'

The other said: 'Well, the way we met was a bit on the painful side for me, but anyway I'm mighty glad to make your acquaintance.' And he gave Sandra a smile composed of friendliness and admiration.

'You're really feeling all right now?' she queried.

He nodded. 'Knocked the wind out of my sails for the moment, but I'm okay now.' He turned to Jimmy. 'Of course, as I expect you've noticed, I'm not exactly what you might call a local boy.' He chuckled and continued; 'No, I'm a few miles away from my hometown all right. New Zealand's where I hail from, little place near Auckland.' He leaned back, a thumb in his waistcoat, his face taking on a reminiscent expression. 'Yes . . . made my little packet — sheep, y'know — and thought I'd like to come over and take a look at the Old Country. Parents were English, North Country folk, as a matter of fact.'

Sandra contrived to look suitably interested and impressed by the fat man's success-story, while Jimmy idly waited for the opportune moment when, without betraying his impatience too obviously, he and Sandra could beat a retreat to the restaurant.

The man from New Zealand was saying: 'By the way, my name's Hodson, Sam Hodson.'

Jimmy introduced Sandra and himself.

'Arrived here yesterday, I did,' the other went on. 'So haven't had much time to see around. But from what I have glimpsed of it, London's quite a town. Eh?'

Jimmy murmured something to the effect that the place had its moments.

'Got a young nephew over here,' Hodson said. 'Only relative I have — y'see, I'm not married.'

'Aren't you?' said Sandra, her eyebrows raised flatteringly to convey she found it difficult to understand how anyone so eligible had managed to keep clear of the scores of designing charmers who must have swarmed around him. Jimmy's glance derisively mocked at her efforts to keep the conversation going. He knew she was bored too, and wanted to beat it to the restaurant as urgently as he did.

Hodson burbled on in his fat voice: 'Yes, Charles — my nephew — is studying to be a chemist. Clever boy, too. Doing well. And I believe me or believe me not, we hadn't met until this morning.

'Course we've corresponded since he was so high.'

Sandra said: 'Really?'

Jimmy followed up with: 'Amazing!'

The other glanced at his opulent-looking watch. 'Just on one. Should be here any minute. Like you to meet him.'

Jimmy realized the chap would feel disappointed and sadly hurt if he and Sandra made their impatience to escape appear too apparent — and he wasn't a bad sort, well-meaning and eagerly anxious to talk to someone in a strange country. At the same time, Jimmy didn't want he and Sandra to get involved in several rounds of drinks with the fat man and his cherished nephew. At that moment he happened to catch the eye of the barman, who was an acquaintance of long standing — or leaning. Hodson being engrossed in giving Sandra further details from his life-story, Jimmy was able to convey by winks, assorted graphic facial expressions, and nods in the direction of the telephone-booth in the corner an indication of the subterfuge he had in mind.

The barman, sharp-witted and imaginative, caught on almost at once. He answered with a sly grin and nod which said: 'Leave it to me, I'll take care of it,' and Jimmy relaxed and left it to him.

He turned back to Sandra and Hodson just as the latter broke off his conversation to call out to a man wearing horn-rims and a wide smile who was approaching: 'Hello, Turner — what are you going to have?'

The man called Turner's smile stretched wider. Hodson muttered to Sandra and Jimmy: 'Friend of mine, met him here last night. We got really pally. Good sort.' And beaming expansively upon the newcomer, who gave him a hearty slap on the shoulder, reiterated: 'What's yours?'

Jimmy caught Sandra's fleeting expression of despair before she replaced it with the same fixed smile she'd been wearing for the last ten tedious minutes.

'I could use a sherry, thanks,' the man in horn-rims was saying to Hodson, who screwed up his face in disapproval of the other's choice of *apéritif*.

'Sherry, bah! Never drink it — '

'No?' was the smiling response. 'Sherry before lunch — or dinner — port afterwards, one of my rules.'

'Port — filthy stuff! Never drink it. You ought to stick to this' — indicating his glass and Jimmy's, to whom he looked for agreement. 'Eh?'

Jimmy shrugged. 'One man's treat is another man's poison,' he smiled. The fat man chortled and the other's eyes twinkled behind his glasses. Hodson ordered his drink from the waiter, then introduced Sandra and Jimmy, launching into a description of the circumstances of their meeting with him outside the hotel. He had reached the end of his account, when a youngish man strode briskly towards them from the direction of the lift, and hailed him as 'Uncle'.

Sandra flashed Jimmy a glance of appeal that carried a touch of desperation in it. Her look told him if he didn't get them out of this and make it snappy, she would never have any faith in him again over anything. He grinned back at her reassuringly, before eyeing Hodson's nephew who was being introduced by his uncle in a voice that fairly quivered with pride. His name was Charles Vernon. Jimmy privately thought he was a not particularly prepossessing specimen of young manhood. Maybe it was the too-close set of his eyes or the weak droop of his mouth, but he instantly summed him up as not much good. There was something almost pathetic about the fat man as he eulogistically praised his nephew's qualities.

Any further speculations Jimmy may have indulged in regarding young Vernon, however, were brushed aside by the interruption he had been awaiting arriving in the person of the barman, who had hurried over, his face clouded with a harassed expression.

'Excuse me, sir,' he said to Jimmy, 'but they've just 'phoned down from the restaurant to say Mr. North has been waiting for you over ten minutes.'

Sandra stared at the barman wide-eyed. Then she saw Jimmy reacting as if the message was causing him the gravest concern. He glanced at his watch and clicking his tongue impatiently exclaimed:

'Dear me, I didn't realize it was so late. Ask them to apologize to Mr. North for us and say we're coming right up.'

'Very good, sir.'

The barman bowed gravely, pocketed the tip Jimmy slipped him and hurried off. With raised eyebrows Sandra stared at his departing white-coated back — which seemed to suggest that its owner was concentrated on delivering a message of the most vital importance — and returned her puzzled gaze to Jimmy. He took her arm, giving it a little extra pressure as he turned to the three men.

'Afraid we must be moving,' he said to Hodson, his smile including the other two; 'old friend of mine up from Cornwall — really mustn't keep him waiting any longer.'

'Of course, of course,' the fat man said, using Jimmy's hand like a pump-handle. 'Very glad to have met you, and — ' beaming at Sandra — 'this very charming young lady.'

She beamed back, there followed appropriate murmurings from Turner and the nephew, then Jimmy and Sandra headed like arrows for the lifts. As they waited for the lift-doors to slide together after them, Sandra breathed an eloquently thankful sigh and said: 'I can hardly wait to meet your pal from Cornwall!'

Jimmy's attention seemed attracted for the moment by the liftboy, who appeared not to have noticed them and was deep in rapt contemplation of a small object he was holding.

The youngster, conscious of his look, glanced up at him and said cheekily: 'Crikey! Some fellers gets all the fun, don't they? See what I mean — '

Jimmy found himself regarding a snapshot of two men and two girls. The girls were pretty and pert in the briefest of swimsuits. The men also wore swimsuits and their arms were twined affectionately around the girls' waists, which, by their wide smiles, both lovelies seemed to find eminently enjoyable.

'That young one just dropped it,' the liftboy said, jerking a grimy thumb towards the trio from whom Jimmy and Sandra had just made their escape.

Jimmy said: 'You'd better give it him back. May be a souvenir of his most romantic memory.'

The youngster giggled. 'I'll take you up first,' he said, pushing the snapshot into his pocket, adding with a knowing look: 'Crikey, but I bet he's a one, sir — don't you?'

'Shouldn't wonder,' responded Jimmy, though somewhat absently, 'shouldn't wonder at all.'

The lift bore them smoothly towards the restaurant.

After the waiter had disappeared with their order, Sandra said: 'Frightfully witty of you thinking of Mr. North from Cornwall — but how did the barman know about him too?'

'He's psychic.'

'And — ?' Sandra encouraged him.

'While the fat boy from the sheep-farm was engrossing your attention, I went into a trance.' Jimmy smiled at her tenderly.

She said: 'I was practically sleep-walking myself I was so bored. But do go on . . . So you went into a trance.'

Jimmy pressed a hand to his brow in a

mock dramatic attitude of concentration.

'It's difficult to remember after that,' he murmured, 'everything became misty, dark . . . '

She was laughing now, in that delightfully attractive way of hers, so Jimmy paused and looked at her and forgot the comedy, forgot every little thing except how adorable she was.

'Well, anyway,' she was saying, 'thank heavens the barman was psychic. I was terrified we were going to get involved in the dreariest party — ' She caught his glance and broke off to study him with a quizzical little smile.

She said: 'Which would it be, darling? Do I look like hell, or have you gone into another of your trances?'

'I was just thinking about you.'

'In the nicest kind of way, of course?'

'It always is that way when I think about you.'

She sighed, as if to say it was old stuff and she didn't believe it; but her eyes were bright. He made it sound new and difficult not to believe, the way he said it.

He put his head slightly on one side.

He said: 'Want to know something, darling?'

She said: 'I might as well.'

'That fat geezer and those two with him — something a trifle off-key about 'em.'

'Forgive me, darling,' she said sweetly, 'but you have me just the tiniest bit confused. Your brain's too agile, it gets around so. I thought for the moment I was on your mind, not the fat man.'

'Just remembered noticing the way you kind of recoiled when that nephew character breezed his way in,' he said.

'Was it so obvious as that?'

'I merely happened to catch your first fleeting reaction, that's all. You covered up.'

'Expect my face had got so tired of that fixed smile I'd been wearing, it felt it simply had to be itself for a moment or scream. Anyway, I took a poor view of the nephew — sly-looking piece I thought.'

He nodded.

She said: 'But why are we talking about them? We could talk about the weather, or what we're going to do this afternoon, or — ' She broke off to ask suddenly: 'Jimmy, d'you think he isn't really his nephew, that he's one of those confidence tricksters or something, after the fat man's money that he's made out of all his sheep?'

Jimmy said with certainty: 'He's not a 'con' man.' He didn't think it necessary to add that he knew, by sight and reputation, pretty nearly every operator in London working that line of business, and was in fact acquainted with several of those smooth and polished gentlemen. He added: 'Whether he's a relation or not is something else. Though I imagine old Hodson must have good reasons for believing he is. After all, they've been corresponding with each other for years.'

'That's all right, then,' Sandra said.

Jimmy was about to offer some observation to the effect that there were more ways of polishing-off pussy than popping it down the well, when the waiter halted the *hors-doeuvres* trolley at their table and he at once gave his full attention to the array of dishes and their succulent contents.

17

When presently the waiter pushed off with his trolley, Sandra glanced round the restaurant and remarked:

'Supposing that bright trio come in for lunch in a minute — they can't miss our table — how'll you explain the absence of your impatient pal from Cornwall?'

'Sam Hodson and party won't be lunching here,' said Jimmy easily, as he impaled a portion of anchovy. 'In fact, the old boy never eats in the restaurant, but always in his private sitting room.'

She looked at him with a certain wonderment. 'How on earth d'you know that?'

'The *maitre d'hôtel* murmured the information in my ear when we came in,' he said. 'Foreseeing the possibility you've mentioned, I'd inquired about the chances. That was while you were smiling at the dark, handsome waiter who led you to this table,' he reminded her with a grin.

'Come to mention it, he is somewhat good-looking in a sort of way,' she said. 'Rather your type, only of course nothing like so repellent.'

'I'm glad,' Jimmy said.

She laughed at him, then said: 'You think of practically everything, don't you? Finding out about the fat man, I mean.'

Jimmy didn't reply at once, and Sandra gave him a quick glance from beneath her thick lashes, wondering a little at his faraway expression. But she didn't say anything; he'd only duck the question if he didn't want to answer it, and he'd come back in a minute anyway.

That was how it was with Jimmy Strange.

★　★　★

The following morning:

Jimmy, attired in a dark dressing gown, was sitting down to breakfast. He had just come from under a cold shower preceded by a hot tub, his razor had skimmed his jaw like a dream, there was an inviting aromatic smell of coffee in the air and he felt really good. He glanced idly at the newspaper folded on the table, and picked it up without any special curiosity. The headlines, as usual, were trying their damnedest to make him hit the ceiling with excitement as they leapt up at him from the front page, and he wondered, with casual amusement, if editors honestly believed the screaming scare-type searing the page with daily monotony had the slightest effect on the majority of readers, other than maybe drawing from them a tolerant chuckle or two.

And then halfway down, where the headlines ended and where in the little space remaining, it was possible to read some actual news, he came upon the report of Sam Hodson's death. Just for a second the penny didn't drop, the name didn't ring a bell. Yet in that fraction of time something in his brain clicked, so that when his eyes had narrowed with interest it was as if the news hadn't hit him smack out of a clear sky. It was as if by some queer trick of prophetic vision he'd been expecting to read it.

According to the short account, Hodson had died at his hotel the night before. 'New Zealand Sheep King', he was described as, and Jimmy thought that for once, if unconsciously, the reporter had concocted an exaggeration that would not have displeased the person so described. Old Hodson would no doubt have taken great pride and thoroughly enjoyed the title that had been conferred upon him. His death, the report added, had occurred suddenly, while he was dining with his nephew in his private room. Charles Vernon's version of the tragedy was briefly quoted, and as he read it Jimmy's mouth tightened. Carefully he read the paragraph through again. It said it all right. There in black and white. He stared through the paper, and once again his mind's eye saw the nephew striding across the Regis Hotel American Bar and hailing the fat man. Jimmy was remembering the eyes too close together for anybody's good but Charles Vernon's, plus the weak, greedy droop of the mouth corners.

Jimmy finished his breakfast, lit a cigarette and leaned back to put in some constructive thinking. The 'phone jangled, he lifted the receiver.

'Good morning, darling, and I hope you slept well.'

Sandra, who hadn't spoken, said: 'How did you guess?'

Jimmy said: 'What had I got to lose if it

wasn't you, darling?'

'Quick as a flash you are, even so early in the day.'

'Would you have believed me if I'd said my heart told me it was you?' Jimmy said tenderly.

'No.'

'That's what I thought.' He went on smoothly, 'What's on your mind, Sandra?'

'I've just seen in the paper Sam Hodson died suddenly; remember — the fat man?'

'I remember — the fat man.'

'Poor thing!' she said. 'Gave me quite a shock. I wondered if you'd read about it, too.'

'I read about it.'

'Yes, I might have known you'd have spotted it.' She paused a moment, then said: 'That was all, Jimmy.' And added brightly: 'Well, it's given us something to talk about.'

'There are plenty of other topics I could find to talk over with you.'

'Such as?'

'You'd have to come closer.'

She laughed softly. Then:

'Jimmy, you don't think . . . ? I mean — I suppose it's silly, but how d'you think the poor man died?'

A short silence. He wondered if she'd noticed the significance of the paragraph that quoted Charles Vernon. She took, among others, the same newspaper. He said slowly:

'Meaning just what?'

'Well, that sinister nephew of his, and — ' She broke off with a little laugh. 'Oh, I expect you think I'm just babbling — '

'I'd rather listen to you babbling than anyone else talking sense. You have a very cuddlesome voice.'

'Darling!'

He realized she hadn't seen what he'd seen in that paragraph. He said easily:

'I expect it was just natural causes. After all, he couldn't have been in too good condition, carrying all that weight around with him.'

She agreed, and presently Jimmy hung up.

He lit another cigarette and completed his dressing. His reflection in the mirror, as he carefully brushed his hair and meticulously knotted his tie, was slightly sardonic with a flicker of amusement at the back of his eyes. Outside he walked a little way before hailing a taxi. The driver was one he knew.

'Mornin', sir.'

Jimmy grinned at him.

'Where would you like me chariot ter transport yer this bright morning?' the other inquired. 'If yer'll pardon me putting it so poetical-like.'

'Scotland Yard,' Jimmy said.

'Cripes!' was the somewhat un-poetical response. 'Don't say they've pinched yer at larst?'

'Cut the comedy and get going.'

'Yessir' — and got.

The atmosphere of Inspector Crow's office was already hazy with the smoke from his bubbling pipe, as the detective hunched himself over his desk. Among the various noteworthy features characteristic of Inspector Crow was his chronic inability to sit at his desk. He habitually leaned his ponderous bulk against it, his beetling ginger brows almost sweeping its surface as if engrossed in some tangled skein of mystery that required every atom of his concentration to elucidate. True, there were occasions when the case of which he was in charge did provide as nasty a headache as any Scotland Yard official could wish for anyone else in the building to wear. At the moment, however, Inspector Crow, bowed Atlas-like in his chair, with a shaft of sunlight slanting across his rusty grizzled head so that it glinted like an old brass kettle, was merely going over the routine morning correspondence.

In response to his aggressive barks of invitation, the door opened and admitted Sergeant Warburton. The Inspector glanced up at him with a scowl, and then seemed to bend even lower over his desk again, as if the other's entrance added to the burden of responsibility he bore. Warburton usually waited for his superior to snap at him before he ventured to speak. But on this occasion he advanced into the room with ill-concealed animation on his prim features and said:

'What *do* you think, sir?'

Inspector Crow raised his head wearily and eyed the other with active abhorrence.

'All right,' he said, attempting a grotesque mimicry of the Sergeant's precise tones, 'what *do* I think?'

'Guess who's outside asking to see you,' went on Warburton, undaunted by his somewhat unencouraging reception.

Inspector Crow choked, pushed back his chair and exploded: 'What the ruddy hell's the ruddy idea? Prancing in here like a flaming circus horse and asking me what do I think and guess who! What is this, a ruddy game of postman's knock, or kiss-in-the-ring, or ruddy well what?'

Sergeant Warburton blushed to the back of his neck, pursed his lips disapprovingly before he announced:

'It's Mr. Strange, sir — he's called to see you.'

The other's heavy jaw sagged so abruptly it was almost possible to hear the click of the muscles that hinged it.

'Str — Strange?'

'I thought you'd be surprised, sir,' said Warburton complacently.

'Outside, you say?'

The Sergeant nodded. 'I asked him to wait.'

'What in thunder does that pest want?'

'Well, sir — he — er — that is — '

'Don't stand there mumbling, what's he after? What did he say?'

Warburton hesitated, mumbled, and hesitated again. 'Well — er — he asked to see you, sir — '

'You didn't expect him to ask to see my white-haired old mother, did you?'

The other ignored the sarcasm. 'As a matter of fact, I considered his manner was inclined to flippancy — '

Crow banged his pipe down on the desk and grated through clenched teeth: '*What does he want?*'

Sergeant Warburton coughed uncomfortably. 'Since you ask, sir,' he said, 'Mr. Strange put his request rather crudely — er — well — he asked me was I permitting visitors to view the old rhinoceros today . . . ' He coughed again. 'Naturally I failed to comprehend him, and so he — er — elucidated — '

He broke off to glance anxiously at the

Inspector, who was breathing heavily, his face a startlingly purple shade. With a bellow that rattled the windows in the office, and mouthing horrible threats Crow started for the door. The Sergeant stepped nimbly out of his path. As he reached the door, it suddenly opened, and he pulled up with a jerk, every hair of his ginger eyebrows bristling, his jaw thrust forward like the front of a steamroller.

'Hello,' said Jimmy Strange, leaning negligently against the door-jamb; 'delightful weather we're having.'

He puffed a cloud of smoke from his cigarette and strolled into the room. Eyeing Crow's face, he flashed him his most charming smile and inquired pleasantly: 'Or d'you find it somewhat sultry for the time of year?'

Inspector Crow glowered at him silently, except for a curious whinnying sound that seemed to lodge somewhere at the back of his nose. Then he swung abruptly on his heel and lumbered back to his desk. Sergeant Warburton glanced at him, then at Jimmy and back to the other. As if to fill in the pause that lay somewhat heavily on the air, he crossed and closed the door. Then returned and automatically placed a chair for Jimmy, who gave him an affable nod and sat down. Warburton bit his lower lip, threw a glance at the desk, wondering anxiously if he had perhaps exhibited towards Jimmy an unnecessary attentiveness from his superior's viewpoint. However, Inspector Crow hadn't noticed, or if he had was far too preoccupied to care.

Jimmy leaned forward and tapped his cigarette against the large ashtray on the desk. Crow raised his head and regarded him with an expression that contrived successfully to combine a weary tolerance with an implacable hostility.

'Go on,' he said, the sarcasm falling from his lips lightly as a sack of coals, 'make yourself at home.'

'Charmingly hospitable of you,' Jimmy murmured. He reclined lazily in his chair and went on: 'Glad I found you in.'

'Pleasure's entirely yours.'

Jimmy smiled and continued imperturbably: 'I felt I just had to know how you were in health.'

Crow gave a grunt. He picked up his cold pipe in his thick fingers and slowly filled it with a black, evil-looking tobacco, tamping it down into the worn, crusted bowl.

Watching him, Jimmy observed: 'Now this should be interesting. I've never seen anyone smoke liquorice before.'

The other grunted again, but said nothing. Carefully he lit up. When it was drawing satisfactorily, he leaned back heavily in his chair and said: 'Now, Mr. Smartie, if it's not troubling you too much, perhaps you'd be good enough to explain exactly why you've called. Apart from the reason you've already given, which is just your idea of being funny.'

Jimmy produced the report of Sam Hodson's death, which he'd clipped from the newspaper and passed it over to Crow. The Inspector took it and glowered at it suspiciously. He read it through carefully, placed it thoughtfully on his desk. He tried to appear enigmatic for the clipping conveyed absolutely nothing to him. At the same time, he knew it must have some significance, otherwise Jimmy Strange wouldn't have taken the trouble to draw his attention to it, Whatever his opinion of Jimmy Strange from most angles — an opinion which was regrettably practically unrepeatable, certainly unprintable, nevertheless he held an unreserved if grudging admiration for him in one respect. He knew his underworld, and the Inspector had learned to put his shirt on any tip he handed out without so far catching a cold. Which was extremely useful to Inspector Crow. Now while Jimmy watched him amusedly and Sergeant Warburton edged forward and craned his neck to examine the newspaper cutting, the Inspector tried to figure out what in hell it added up to. After a ponderous silence, during which he totted up precisely nothing, he said with a noncommittal growl: 'And what am I supposed to do about it?'

'Unbutton those ears, Big Chief Bull-Face,' Jimmy said, 'and Laughing Water will bang it out for you on the war drums.'

Crow snorted but listened.

Jimmy told him crisply and graphically how he and Sandra had met Sam Hodson outside the Regis Hotel, of their subsequent sojourn to the American Bar, of how the man in horn-rims had joined the party, of Charles Vernon's arrival, introduced by the fat man as his nephew. 'Now,' Jimmy concluded, stubbing out his cigarette, 'take another peek at that clipping, particularly the bit quoting the nephew.'

Crow ran his eye down the account and read aloud:

'Mr. Charles Vernon, nephew of the deceased, describing the tragedy, said, 'My uncle was about to drink a glass of port when he suddenly collapsed and died in my arms' — '

Inspector Crow broke off and glanced sharply at Jimmy. 'Cripes!' he said.

'I hoped you'd catch on,' said Jimmy.

'The deceased having previously declared with emphasis,' Sergeant Warburton observed sententiously, 'that he never indulged in port.'

The Inspector gave him a scowl and, an

inevitable blush suffusing his aesthetic features, the Sergeant subsided. Jimmy grinned up at him in mock wonderment and the other threw him a petulant look.

Followed a silence in the room, except for the rumble of traffic from the Whitehall and the peculiar bubbling noise from Crow's pipe. The detective glanced at the clipping again. 'And then there's this chap what's his name? — Turner,' he mused, fondling his massive chin.

'He could certainly corroborate what Hodson said.' Jimmy nodded.

'He could if he wanted to, you mean?'

'I think I'm having practically no difficulty in following your train of thought.'

'Thing is, where's Turner now?'

Jimmy hesitated a fraction, then shrugged. 'Had the impression he wasn't resident at the Regis. But you'll take care of that.'

'Anyway,' Crow muttered, 'we'll have a little heart-to-heart with this nephew. And a *post-mortem* on Hodson should tell us if he was poisoned.'

Warburton put in: 'Then your opinion, sir, is that poison may have been administered in the port wine by the nephew with the object of bringing about his uncle's demise?'

'Well, he wouldn't slip him a dose of cough-medicine, would he?'

'Quite, sir. And if I may, I would suggest — '

'The day I find myself asking you for a suggestion,' Crow rasped, 'will be the day I quit this ruddy job.'

'Quite, sir, quite — ' Warburton hastily tried to stem the other's rising wrath.

'Until then,' Inspector Crow bellowed remorselessly, '*shut your trap.*'

Jimmy coughed delicately, lit a fresh cigarette and stood up.

'Much as I long to linger amidst this cosy little scene,' he murmured, 'this charming atmosphere of, one might almost say, domestic bliss, I fear I must tear myself away.' With a bow to the Inspector he crossed to the door. 'It's been such an amusing chat,' he went on genially, 'and I know I can leave the matter we've discussed in your hands with complete confidence — *that you'll make a most unholy hash of it.*' And with a parting smile and: 'So long, flattie,' he was gone.

★   ★   ★

Some time later he turned into the Regis Hotel and strolled casually to the lift.

'American Bar.'

'Yessir.' It was the same liftboy who'd been on duty that morning when he and Sandra had encountered Sam Hodson, now deceased. As the lift descended he recognized Jimmy and said perkily: 'Oh, it's you, sir. Good morning.'

Jimmy gave him a friendly nod. 'By the way,' he said casually, 'that snapshot you picked up, remember? You wouldn't by any chance have forgotten to return it to the chap who dropped it?'

The boy grinned at him. 'You mean that snap of the two gents and the two beauts?'

Jimmy inclined his head.

'Why?' the kid asked.

'Nothing really. Only if giving it back to him had slipped your mind — I'm sure you must be kept pretty busy, run off

35

your feet in fact — I think I know someone who might have liked to buy it.'

The other regarded him, head on one side speculatively.

'Now you come to mention it,' he said, as if calling to mind a matter that had somehow escaped his attention, 'I do believe — how much would your friend give for it?'

Jimmy took out a note from his wallet and said: 'Would this do?'

The youngster's mouth opened. Then he wiped the expression of pleasurable anticipation off his face and replaced it with a sly leer. 'Make it two,' he said.

Jimmy smiled gently and, with what seemed to be a single, swift movement, firmly pinched the other's nose and a moment later stepped back, the snapshot in his hand. He pocketed it, while the liftboy, gingerly rubbing his nose, blinked at him with incredulous watering eyes. Jimmy flicked him a coin. 'For being greedy,' he said, as the lift stopped and he stepped out.

He was about to proceed straight to the bar with the idea of manhandling a large

Scotch when a figure rose from a table in his path. Jimmy recognized him and a gleam of elation lit his narrowed eyes. The man moved towards him excitedly and grabbed his arm. Jimmy didn't like anyone to do that, believing in having both hands free at all times. Glancing down at the other's hand he said: 'This arm belongs to Daddy.'

The man released his hold with an apologetic smile.

'This is unbelievable luck,' he said. 'You're the one person I want to see and the last I ever hoped to.'

Jimmy regarded him quizzically.

'As it happens,' he said, 'our wishes could be mutual.'

'I've been wondering how the devil I could find you. And when I saw you walk in you could've knocked me down with a feather.' He nodded towards a corner. 'Let's sit over there, it's — er — quiet.'

He led the way, turning to signal a waiter. They sat down and after the waiter had taken the order Jimmy said: 'Why the hush-hush?'

'If you knew what I do,' was the

response, 'you wouldn't want to shout it from the rooftops, either.'

'Don't tell me,' Jimmy said softly, 'you know who bumped off Sam Hodson?'

The man called Turner stared at him as if he was seeing a ghost. His eyes blinked shortsightedly behind his horn-rims.

'By cripes,' he gasped. 'How did you — ?' He broke off as the waiter approached with the drinks. He was the first to grab his and take a long gulp. Jimmy, eyeing him over the rim of his own glass, saw that his hand was shaking. Turner put his drink down with a sigh, took out his cigarette case and extended it to Jimmy, who, seeing the contents were a Turkish brand, shook his head. The other took one for himself, tapped it nervously on his case, lit it and leaned across the table.

'Now, listen,' he said in a low voice, 'I don't know how much you've twigged about all this, but I'm putting my cards on the table. I'm going to take you into my confidence.' He paused for a moment as if something ironically amusing had suddenly occurred to him. Then he went on. 'Obviously you read about poor old Hodson fading out, and it seems after your comment just now there was one little thing in the newspaper report which also struck yon as odd.'

'I'm not laying down my hand yet,' Jimmy told him.

Turner drew back at the thrust and gave a wry grimace. Then he shrugged.

'Okay,' he said. 'But I'll ask you if you remember something that happened yesterday morning — right here in this very bar? When Hodson asked me to name my drink.'

Jimmy's expression was blandly vague.

'I'll refresh your memory,' the other said obligingly, leaning closer.

'Go right ahead.'

'When Hodson asked me what mine was I said it was a sherry. And he said he hated the stuff.' Jimmy permitted a glimmering of recollection to begin to animate his features. Encouraged, his companion continued: 'And even went on to say he thought port was a foul drink, too — now does it come back to you?' — he bit the words out with emphasis

— 'and never drank the stuff.'

'It rings a bell now you mention it,' Jimmy said.

Turner gave him a gimlet look from behind his glasses. 'I'm glad of that,' he said, 'because when I draw your attention to this — in case you didn't notice it before' — Jimmy let the sarcastic edge blunt itself against him by appearing unaware of it, while the other drew a newspaper clipping from his pocket — 'you'll get what I'm driving at.'

Jimmy at once perceived the clipping to be a report of Hodson's death similar to the one he had seen earlier. Though cut from another newspaper it was in fact practically word for word what he had already read for himself. Turner's forefinger pointed out the significant quotation. Jimmy gave a creditable impersonation of someone overcome with shocked surprise.

'Hell's bells,' he exclaimed, 'why hadn't that struck me?'

Studied disbelief that it hadn't was in the other's stare. Then he shrugged as if to convey that Jimmy's pretended obtuseness was neither here nor there anyway and said, his voice slightly hoarse with the weight of his observation: 'Only you and I, apart from Vernon himself, of course, know he murdered his uncle.'

Jimmy refrained from observing: 'Only the three of us, plus Scotland Yard.' Instead he contrived to look suitably impressed. Turner tapped the ash off his Turk, the stub of which was discoloured and soggy, glanced cautiously round to reassure himself no one was within earshot and Jimmy waited for him to unload. He had a pretty good idea of the lines along which the other's heart-to-heart piece would run.

'Listen,' the man was telling him across the table, 'I'm giving it you straight. I met Hodson the night before last for the first time. It was in this bar.' He hesitated, then went on. 'Now, you might as well know it. I used to be in the — er — well, the Castle-in-Spain line, gold brick racket, sunken treasure gag — whatever you like to call it. You'd be surprised how many mugs fall for the old stuff, though of course I was subtle, I gave it a fresh twist. Are you with me?'

'I'm right alongside.'

'Okay. Well, anyway, a little while ago I fall for the oldest confidence trick in the world myself. Yes, believe me, I meet a girl and I want to marry her.' He gave a little laugh. 'Imagine it!'

Jimmy preferred not to imagine it, but didn't say anything and the other proceeded. 'But when she comes to realize my — er — profession she begs me to quit. And I'm with her all the way. I want to quit too. I want to settle down with a comfortable income from strictly on the level sources. But where's the dough coming from? You need capital to set yourself up and I'd never thought much about the rainy day and money in the old sock. So I'm turning all this over in my mind and then, night before last like I told you, this Hodson egg buys me a drink. Well, when a real live New Zealand Sheep King starts putting out the welcome sign and telling me his life-story just as if we're old-time buddies, can you blame me if I say to myself here's the cash I need waiting, just waiting for the milking?'

'I see your point of view,' Jimmy told him.

'Anyway, to cut a long story to the bare outlines, I went to it and gave him a really sweet little bedtime yarn. He bites at it like a hungry pike, hook, line and fishing rod.' He sighed regretfully,

'Had him landed for thousands — then his nephew goes and croaks him.'

There was a pause. Jimmy was admitting to himself Turner's yarn was somewhat franker — up to a point — than he'd been expecting. Not that it made any essential difference to the setup. It merely indicated the other realized, as things were, the more convincing his account of his meeting with Hodson the better. Even if it meant revealing himself in a not exactly pearly light.

Jimmy murmured: 'You seem pretty sure Vernon did it.'

The other nodded, lit another cigarette from his used stub. 'This is the way I see it,' he said, crushing the butt into a mess in the ashtray. 'Vernon — he's a chemist, don't forget, so he should know all the poison tricks — dopes the old boy's glass

43

of whisky. Whisky, see? Then, when Hodson's kicked the bucket he washes out the glass so's . . . there'll be no trace of the poison. Vernon's smart and to make it look natural and fit in with the story he's going to tell he doesn't want it to be empty. But he makes a slip, because what does he do? He refills the glass with *port*, which he was drinking himself, not knowing, or forgetting his uncle never touched the stuff.'

Jimmy, who had already formed in his own mind this reconstruction of what had occurred, looked thoughtful, then nodded his head in agreement. 'Certainly seems that's about the way it went.'

'You bet. And if you need a motive to make it stick — Vernon is his uncle's sole heir. Hodson told me that himself.' He leaned forward again. 'What other explanation could there be for the port being there?' He indicated the newspaper clipping. 'The old boy wouldn't touch it with a bargepole. So how comes it's in his glass? His nephew.'

He sat back and finished off his drink. Jimmy signalled the waiter, and when the drinks had been brought, the other shifted a little restlessly in his chair before he began talking again.

'You see,' he muttered tentatively, 'I — well — of course, I ought to go to the cops. But it's tricky for me. I've got a record. And they won't say to themselves I was pally with Hodson just because I liked the colour of his blue eyes. So I'm in a kind of a spot. They'll pinch Vernon for the murder, but they'll pinch me too, for the little game I was playing — even though I never actually pulled anything off. I'd take a chance and spin 'em a stanza, but — ' He shrugged off the idea as one that would prove utterly unacceptable to the police. 'So you see how it is? I reckon Vernon oughtn't to get away with it, but what can I do to stop him?'

Jimmy only offered: 'Naturally you want to keep your nose clean.' And waited with inward and somewhat sardonic amusement for what was coming next . . . Turner nervously knocked a negligible amount of ash from his cigarette, waiting for a word of encouragement, which wasn't forthcoming. So said:

'But you *could* tip the cops.'

Jimmy simulated surprise. 'How?'

'Don't you know as much as I do?' the other urged him. 'Why can't you go to Scotland Yard, tell 'em what you've read in the paper and how you know Hodson never drank port? You're right in the clear, you'd be all right.'

Jimmy considered for a moment. Then: 'Why should I? What's in it for me?'

Turner blinked at him as if his finer sensibilities were faintly outraged. 'There isn't anything in it for either of us,' he expostulated. 'That's not the idea. Not the idea at all.'

'What would be the idea?'

'Well, it's simply a question of not letting a murderer get away with it.'

'Vernon hasn't murdered you or me.'

'No, but — well, I mean — it's a matter of principle. Moral principle.' He seemed to experience a certain difficulty in getting the word off his teeth. As if the sentiment was a little out of his line.

'I get it.' Jimmy smiled at him thinly. 'You've gone all high-minded. Pardon me if I wasn't exactly in step with you. I imagined you were just out for revenge.'

Turner shifted uncomfortably in his chair. Then he grinned broadly. 'Okay,' he admitted. 'Supposing it is just that. Vernon did me out of thousands. All the same, he's still a dirty killer, and you ought to want to see him swing.'

There was that faraway expression in Jimmy's eyes.

'Besides,' the other was continuing, 'if I were placed like you — with nothing to lose — I wouldn't like to feel I was withholding important information from the police.'

'Vernon was a stranger to you, you say?'

Turner nodded emphatically. 'Never set eyes on him before yesterday. Why?'

'I was just wondering, perhaps it wouldn't be a bad notion to look him up, have a chat. Maybe you know where I might find him?'

'The hotel can put you on to that — but I don't see where it'd get you. And you might say something which would make him suspicious, scare him off.'

'He'd stick around until the will was settled.'

'Not if you put it into his bean you were on to him. Be a damn' sight too anxious to save his skin to worry over anything else.'

Jimmy seemed to think round the point and after a moment nodded agreement. 'Maybe you're right.' He brushed some flakes of cigarette ash off his coat and stood up. 'Might as well make a move now.'

'You're going to the police?'

Jimmy nodded. The other was on his feet.

'You'll keep me out of this, won't you?' he said anxiously.

'Take it easy.'

'Okay. I'll stick around if you like till you get back. Then you can wise me how they react.'

'I was going to ask you where I could get in touch with you.'

'I'll be here.' And Turner sat down again.

Jimmy bestowed one of his most charming smiles upon him and went out of the bar. Gaining Piccadilly, he paused unobtrusively in a doorway and lit a cigarette, never taking his eyes off the hotel. He remained there watching for several minutes. Then, satisfied the man in horn-rims hadn't planned to beat it after he'd left him, but was, as he'd suggested, awaiting his return, Jimmy grabbed a taxi.

He was back within twenty minutes, accompanied by Inspector Crow and Sergeant Warburton, hovering in the background, and regarding the surroundings of the American Bar with prim disapproval. To say Turner was considerably taken aback by the approach of Jimmy's two companions would be an understatement. He was not too surprised, however, to leap up and make a dash for it. Crow lumbered forward to close with him, but the man was as resourceful as he was agile. He managed to hook his foot round the Inspector's ankle and send him sprawling into the arms of Sergeant Warburton, as the latter rushed forward to lend assistance. With a thin smile of amusement at the slightly incongruous spectacle of Crow sagging in Warburton's arms, Jimmy stood between

Turner and the glass swing doors of the wide stairway ascending to the street level. As Turner rushed him, Jimmy stood carefully to one side and deftly flicked the other's glasses off his nose. The man gave a yelp of blind despair and collided with a table. He was still pushing myopically at a large mirror, under the mistaken impression it was the way out, when Crow and the Sergeant pounced on him. After that he said he would go quietly.

★ ★ ★

'They picked up Vernon all right, of course,' Jimmy told Sandra over a drink at her flat some time later. 'Blustered and threatened all sorts of nasty things for the old Crow, he did, for detaining him. Quite convincing he made it sound, I understand. Busy with his studies, important work, and he couldn't tell him any more about his uncle's death than anyone could read in the newspapers, that it'd been a heart attack. I think Vernon hinted rather broadly perhaps Crow couldn't read — ' Jimmy broke off and chuckled.

'Did he try to hide that he was Hodson's sole heir?' Sandra asked.

'Not a bit. Asked if being a sole heir constituted a crime, if so, was it something new, because he'd never heard of it before.'

'Inspector Crow must have loved him,' Sandra said.

'It didn't get him any place. Crow just stuck at him like the old rhinoceros he is and suddenly Vernon cracked. Went bang off the handle in a fit of hysterics. Shouted that if Crow knew so much he might as well know the lot. Then asked politely to be allowed to make a statement. And as statements go, it couldn't have gone much further.'

'He admitted he'd done it?'

Jimmy nodded. 'Full confession. He'd concocted the dope, which apart from its immediate deadly effect, produced the signs of heart failure. Described how he administered it in Hodson's whisky — '

'Exactly the way the other man — Turner — had told you,' Sandra said.

'Word for word.' Jimmy smiled. 'And who should have been able to give a better running commentary, so to speak, if he couldn't.'

She looked at him questioningly.

'The nephew's statement implicated Turner as accessory. According to Vernon it was the other who'd suggested the idea and worked it out.'

Sandra was wide-eyed.

'Turner didn't deny it,' Jimmy went on, amused at her incredulity.

'They were going fifty-fifty over the proceeds. And if Vernon hadn't bungled it by refilling Hodson's glass with port instead of whisky, chances are they'd have got away with it.'

'I suppose,' Sandra found her voice, 'when he saw the bit in the paper about the drink, he was afraid you might notice it too and wonder. That's why he told you that story in the hotel, pinning the whole thing on to Vernon?'

'He felt his buddy had dropped the brick so he could carry the baby. Quite a natural way of looking at it from his slant.'

Sandra shuddered a little. 'What a horrible pair!'

'Choice couple,' Jimmy agreed.

She glanced at him suddenly.

'Come to think of it,' she said slowly, 'you haven't explained why you suspected Turner of being mixed up in it.'

'Come to think of it, I haven't.'

'How did you guess he knew the other one all the time and his story was a pack of lies?'

He grinned at her over his glass.

'Come on,' she said, 'what are you hiding up your sleeve?'

He shook his head. 'Not up my sleeve,' he said, 'in my pocket,' producing the snapshot he'd got from the liftboy. 'His nibs the nephew dropped it in the lift, the morning we met him.'

And Sandra found herself looking at the two pert, pretty, unprotesting young girls in the embrace of the two affectionate young men. One being Charles Vernon, the other Turner.

2

The Judge's Daughter

The jury files back.

Every eye is on them as they reach their seats, the shuffle of their footsteps sounding startlingly clear in the heavy silence of the Old Bailey courtroom. There is a pause. Someone coughs. Tension is at snapping point. A woman, without taking her eyes off the jury, fumbles in her handbag for some smelling salts.

There is a rustle of documents pushed aside and the Clerk of the Court stands up, nervously fiddling with his pince-nez. In a dry, thin voice he asks:

'Gentlemen of the Jury, have you considered your verdict?'

The foreman, round-faced, with beads of perspiration starting on his brow, licks his lips. His voice is scarcely audible.

'We have.'

Pause.

Then slowly that thin, dry voice frames the words:

'Do you find James Benson guilty or not guilty?'

A long, deathly silence.

The foreman's low-voiced but firm response:

'Guilty.'

And the woman with the smelling salts suddenly tipping forward, uttering a faint moan as she falls into an inert heap. A shuddering gasp seems to move over the Court like an icy wind from the Valley of Death itself, and attention now is divided between the suddenly sagging figure in the dock and the macabre motions of the judge as he places the black cap on his head. So that the Clerk of the Court's query is almost lost.

'Prisoner at the bar, you stand convicted of murder. Have you anything to say why the Court should not give you judgment according to the law?'

No answer from the dock. No indication that the question has been heard.

Now Mr. Justice Henderson leans forward, his face as ashen as his wig. Precisely, unemotionally, his words fall, his eyes never waver from the man before him.

'James Benson, you have been convicted of this brutal crime upon the clearest evidence. Throughout your trial you have shown not the slightest indication that you have felt any emotions of remorse; rather have you exhibited the same callous inhumanity that characterizes the murder you committed.' A slight, almost imperceptible pause. Then: 'It is my duty to direct that you be removed from this Court to a place of confinement for twenty-one days, when you shall be taken forth and hanged by the neck until you are dead . . .'

★ ★ ★

Coincidence notoriously pulls a fast one at times.

Occasionally, indeed, its long arm stretches out to waggle the strings of Fate and set certain puppets dancing against each other to such calculated dramatic effect that a sceptical eyebrow is apt to be raised, and even coincidence considered to have gone too far.

Notwithstanding, no less a sceptic than Jimmy Strange was content to reckon the night he turned his car along by Hampstead Heath, and narrowly missed running down Mr. Justice Henderson's daughter, was demonstrably one of the long-armed goddess's big-time acts put on for his especial benefit.

Until that moment, the dual facts that he happened to have attended the Benson trial, and with Sandra happened to have lunched recently at a certain little Soho restaurant renowned for its ravioli, might forever have remained as unrelated to each other as they were, by themselves, insignificant.

The other fact that the judge's daughter looked indubitably attractive by moonlight had, so Jimmy assured Sandra, nothing whatever to do with the case.

As to what he was doing driving by the Heath at that time of night he remained reticently vague. Sandra was disinclined to accept his bland explanation that he'd merely taken the car out because it had been cooped up all day and he'd thought it needed a run.

But to come to the night in question.

Jimmy was cruising along at a reasonable lick, casually admiring the moonlit panorama of the Heath stretching away on his right. On his left, detached houses of various shapes and sizes stood back from the road, some of them partially screened by fences and hedges, others almost completely hidden by trees.

He noticed the car absently as he approached, parked outside the gates of one of the houses and in the shade of some tall trees. He didn't see the girl until she suddenly stepped out of the shadows and from behind the car, waving at him to stop.

He braked and admonished her:

'And I suppose if I'd knocked you for six you'd have had me pinched for dangerous driving.' He shook his head gravely. 'Suddenly running out like that made my heart turn cartwheels.'

'I'm so sorry,' she said breathlessly. 'I

only just heard you coming along and was afraid I mightn't stop you.'

Her voice was nice, cool and low.

He regarded her and said through what he hoped was a devastating smile: 'I'd have stopped for you if Old Nick himself'd been on my tail.'

Her response was a half-smile, however. He guessed she was thinking he might be one of the troublesome type and had perhaps made a mistake in asking his help.

'Cheer up,' he said. 'It was the sort of remark the nicest man would have made.'

She laughed then and her expression cleared.

'What's the trouble?' he asked.

'I can't get the car to start. I think the battery must be run down.'

'Too bad. What d'you want me to do about it?'

'Give me a lift, if you will, please. I live only a mile away, but I must get back quickly.'

'What about your car?'

'I can 'phone a garage when I get home.'

'Let's go, then.'

He held the door open and she got in. She wore a fur coat over an evening frock and her shoes were silvery coloured and fragile.

'It's very kind of you,' she said as the car accelerated. 'I'm not really dressed for walking, and goodness knows when I'd have got a taxi.'

'Driving back from a party, or something?'

'Not exactly. Matter of fact, I've got quite a party of my own on, or supposed to have.' She added with a kind of hesitant shyness: 'It's my twenty-first birthday.'

'Many happy returns.'

'Thank you. My aunt was there and wasn't feeling too good — she's not very strong — so I slipped away to run her home. When I got into the car to come back, it wouldn't budge.'

'And that's where I came in.'

She laughed. 'I suppose it was rather risky, in a way, stopping a stranger for a lift, but I felt pretty anxious, leaving the party flat and all that. Anyway,' giving him a sidelong glance, 'I was lucky.'

He inclined his head in acknowledgement, a smile quirking his lips. Then said:

'Maybe your father mightn't agree. I imagine he'd want to hear more evidence first, before — er — pronouncing judgment.'

She looked at him quickly.

'You know who I am?'

He nodded. 'Often see your picture when I get a haircut — in the smart magazines.' Quoting: ' 'Miss Margot Henderson, lovely daughter of Mr. Justice Henderson — and friend'.'

She gave a little laugh and said: 'Awful nonsense, isn't it?'

He shrugged non-committally, his eyes on the road. 'Plenty of people have had grimmer captions under their photos. Take those under the face that was splashed all over the papers last Sunday. Not a pretty face, true, in fact I personally found it distinctly repulsive.'

'You mean Benson' — shuddering a little. Then a slight frown marked her brow as if an idea had suddenly occurred to her. 'I wonder if . . . ?' she murmured

61

to herself, then broke off. 'No, of course, it couldn't be . . . '

'Something on your mind?'

She jerked her head up, apparently not realizing she'd been musing aloud.

'Oh, no, it's — it's nothing.'

He threw her a glance. Saw that her smile was somewhat forced and that an anxious shadow remained in her eyes. She was saying conversationally;

'Were you by any chance at the Benson trial?'

'So you think I look the sort who might be interested in that type of entertainment?'

'Well, all kinds of people were there. Actors and novelists, and so on.'

'And which would you take me for, actor or author?'

She regarded his profile above his impeccable evening shirt and black tie with mock seriousness.

'You could be either, I suppose,' she said dubiously. 'But somehow I'd say you were someone quite different.'

'You've got something there,' he grinned at her.

'Oh, here we are,' she said suddenly. 'This house we're coming to.'

He pulled up outside tall gates, beyond which the house, large and rambling, stood at the end of a short drive. There were a number of cars parked along the drive, and from within dance music could be heard.

'Sounds fun,' Jimmy said. 'Though I can't imagine Mr. Justice Henderson joining the frivolity.'

'Father's a very good dancer, as a matter of fact. He's an old darling, too!'

'Glad to hear it. I must admit he looked pretty grim at the Old Bailey.'

'So you *were* there?' — looking at him speculatively. 'You know, I believe you have quite an air of mystery about you.' And then suddenly; 'You — you — aren't a detective, are you?'

He gave a chuckle. It died on his lips as something in her voice caused him to glance at her sharply.

'You sounded as if you wished I *were* a dick — er — detective,' he said.

She didn't say anything. Only the shadow was there in her eyes.

He could see it, though she wasn't looking at him, she was looking at the house.

He said: 'Personally I find it very cosy, sitting here in the moon-glow with you, but hadn't you better be popping in? They'll be wondering what's happening to you.'

She turned to him. 'You'll think I'm a little fool.' Her voice was cool and low. 'But there's something about you makes me feel you could help me.'

He sighed and nodded. Said amiably: 'I often look that way to people in the moonlight.'

She didn't smile.

He said: 'What d'you want to know?'

She said: 'I'm frightened.'

He surveyed her for a moment, then took out his cigarette case, flipped it open and extended it to her. 'Nothing like a cigarette when you're scared stiff — I always use one.'

She took one abstractedly. Through a cloud of cigarette smoke he said; 'Is it anything to do with the Benson business?'

The girl caught her breath and stared at him.

'What made you say that?'

He shrugged. 'Shot in the dark.'

She said quickly: 'I hadn't thought of it before, but when you mentioned it just now I suddenly wondered — ' She broke off and took out a letter from her handbag.

'This came this morning. It — it — well, it could be quite amusing.'

He read:

Dear Miss Henderson,

This is what I write is warning you are in danger. Someone who I cannot say swear he kills you because for your father. Please I tell you this no joke.

A well-wisher.

He handed the letter back to her, and she said:

'It's a foreigner, of course. But what extraordinary writing. All squiggles and squirls.'

'Woman's, I'd say.' He drew at his cigarette and exhaled thoughtfully.

'D'you think . . . ?' she began, and left the query in the air, her eyes searching his anxiously.

'Can't say that sort of letter has me doubled up exactly with merriment.'

'You mean there may be something to it?'

He leaned forward and said with easy familiarity: 'Listen, Margot, you've got a sweet face, and I bet you dance like a dream. They tell me I'm no camel, so what are we waiting for?'

She looked somewhat taken aback.

He chuckled and went on: 'You asked me to help you. All right. So I will. But it isn't all done with mirrors. I don't work magic. Catch on? I need to think it out. And,' nodding towards the house, 'in there, with you in my arms and an earful of music, I could think plenty.' He paused, then added earnestly: 'Maybe I could get a drink, too.'

She drew a deep breath.

'I must admit I find you almost irresistible!' she said.

The obvious answer was put on the tip of his tongue. The sort of answer she might have expected from him. Which was why, because he could be something of a psychologist when the moment

66

demanded it, he said instead: 'Let's leave my personal charm out of this; what you *really* want to find is the writer of that.' He indicated the letter.

Her expression became serious again.

'Come in and have a drink, please.'

Her voice was quietly casual, but he knew he'd impressed her. He parked the car and they went into the house.

Shortly after being introduced to her father and several people whose names didn't mean a thing in his life, he spotted someone who caused him to raise an eyebrow in quizzical interest.

It happened just after the girl had left him on his own for a few minutes while she chatted to various guests. Which had been all right by Jimmy, who'd promptly found himself a secluded corner of the buffet and proceeded to put in some steady drinking.

Over the rim of his glass he'd a view of part of the hall and the wide staircase. And it was the appearance of a familiar form heavily descending the stairs that caused him to finish off his drink at a gulp and make his way into the hall.

'Well, well, if it isn't the old bird himself,' he said pleasantly. 'And all got up in his fine feathers.'

Detective-Inspector Crow, who was doing his best not to look self-conscious in his evening clothes, stared at Jimmy in open-mouthed surprise. He glowered silently at him for a moment, then, his face twisting sourly, he growled inelegantly:

'Cripes, *you*!'

Jimmy looked pained. 'Really,' he grimaced, 'How does one converse with persons who're obviously unused to moving in the rarefied atmosphere of Society's upper crust?'

Crow snarled: 'I'd like to know what finger you've got in the ruddy pie?'

'Since we speak in metaphors,' Jimmy smiled, 'it's my little finger. Around which I happened to have wrapped the delectable daughter of his nibs.'

'She must be cracked.'

'She is about me.'

'Bah!' the other grunted contemptuously.

'Granted,' Jimmy murmured, then,

eyeing the other through a puff of cigarette smoke, hazarded: 'Did you get a letter, too?'

Crow jumped as if someone had stuck a pin in him. He drew his ginger brows together till they looked like overhanging cliffs. 'How the hell did you know?'

Jimmy grinned. His guess had scored a bull. He went on:

'Written by a foreigner, a woman. Doubtless even your limited intelligence grasped that. Writing somewhat ornamental.'

The Inspector said with feeling: 'I'd like to break your ruddy neck.'

'An entertaining notion, I'm sure — from your point of view. But a trifle shortsighted, don't you think? I mean, killing the goose that lays the golden eggs.'

Crow scowled.

'What else d'you know?' he growled reluctantly.

Jimmy regarded the tip of his cigarette. His expression was profound, but to himself he was wishing he did know more. Not that he'd have passed it on to the Inspector at this stage, of course. He'd learned something, however, as a result of his encounter with the detective. The writer of the letter to the girl had also tipped off Scotland Yard. Which meant, also, Mr. Justice Henderson must know about the whole business; Crow couldn't be here otherwise. But neither he nor the judge had any idea the girl had received a similar warning. Jimmy felt it was time he had another drink and then find the girl. The thought of holding her close while they danced was all right.

He said to Crow:

'Stick around awhile, and I'll keep you posted.'

He was gone, leaving the Inspector glaring after him with an expression which, to put it mildly, might be described as malevolent. His sulphurous ruminations were broken into by the delicate approach of Sergeant Warburton, who made his appearance from the direction of the servants' quarters. He paused beside his superior and observed:

'I must say it's extremely gratifying to meet persons who, though admittedly of only domestic status, are nevertheless cooperative and eminently civil.'

Crow turned a baleful eye on him.

'Stop humming in my ear like a blasted buzz-saw! Have you had a word with the servants, got anything out of 'em — without letting 'em know why we're here?'

'I did precisely that, sir. I have to report they gave no hint of information which might be useful to us.'

The other grunted non-committally.

Head on one side, Warburton eyed him solicitously. 'Has anything occurred to upset you, sir, during my absence?' he asked.

Crow's massive cleft chin stuck out so that his lower lip almost met his nose.

'Strange has turned up,' he muttered.

The Sergeant's eyes popped incredulously. 'Jimmy Strange, did you say, sir?'

'Your hearing's improving.'

'But — but what's he doing here?'

'Knows something about this damned letter business.'

'Well, really now! Quite an irrepressible person, isn't he, sir?'

Crow glared at him, and the other's enthusiasm subsided.

'He's a ruddy nuisance! Butting in on other people's business when it's no concern of his. One of these days . . . ' And the Inspector lapsed into a horrid mumbling as he chewed over the dark fate, he promised himself, he would one day visit upon Mr. Strange.

Meanwhile Jimmy, who would have remained untroubled even had he been aware of the treat Inspector Crow had in store for him, was, with the philosophy characteristic of him, blissfully enjoying the moment in hand. Or, to be more precise, in his arms.

Gazing with undivided concentration into her bright eyes as they danced to the latest sentimental hit from Tin Pan Alley, he murmured to Margot:

'You know, you dance just as deliciously as you look as if you would — if I make myself clear.'

'I think I get the idea!' she laughed at him.

After a moment, when his attention seemed to have strayed, she said: 'By the way, you haven't told me yet what I'm to do about the letter.'

He said: 'Maybe I will — later.'

Something in his voice made her glance at him quickly.

'What *are* you staring at?'

Without looking at her he answered levelly: 'Waiter over there. Little grey-haired chap.'

She turned her head. 'Oh, yes . . . He looks rather ill.'

He nodded in agreement.

The music stopped and she said: 'Shall we have a drink?'

He said: 'You say the cutest things.'

At the buffet he caught her staring at him, her lovely eyes slightly narrowed.

'What's on your mind?' he said.

'Only you intrigue me a little. Who are you, really? What do you do?'

He chuckled. 'Not worrying about the silver are you?'

The barman handed them their drinks. Jimmy raised his glass to her. 'I looks towards you,' he said.

Her baffled expression vanished as their glasses clinked, and she laughed. They paused over her drink to exclaim suddenly: 'You're looking right *past* me!'

He didn't shift his glance from somewhere beyond her shoulders. His steady gaze was sharply speculative. 'Our friend approaches,' he said slowly.

'Who?'

'The waiter.'

She swung round as the man hurried up to her.

'Excuse me, miss — '

'Yes?'

'Your father says he'd like to see you for a minute in the library.'

'Oh . . .'

The man indicated the silver tray he was carrying. 'I'm just taking him some whisky.'

While the barman promptly poured out the drink and put it on the tray, the girl said: 'Very well, tell him I'll be right along.'

'Yes, miss.'

As the waiter hurried away, she turned to Jimmy questioningly. 'What's so odd about him, except he does look awfully ill?'

He said casually: 'It was just an idea I had.'

'Well, perhaps you'll tell me about it when I come back? Can't think what Father wants, but I won't be long.' Then: 'I suppose it's safe for me to leave you?'

He glanced at her sharply.

'I mean you won't run away?' Smiling.

He shook his head. 'Much too — interested.'

After she'd gone he pushed his glass over to the barman. There was a thoughtful frown creasing his brow as he moved his replenished glass round in little circles before he took a drink.

Two men came in; they were laughing and joking over someone they'd obviously just left.

'Where's the old boy got to now?' one of them was chortling.

'I just saw him sneaking off with the judge to the billiard-room.'

Jimmy shot a look at the second speaker, who was continuing: 'Going to show him some new trick-shot or something.'

His companion nodded indulgently.

'Just like a couple of schoolboys they are . . . '

Without waiting to hear any more Jimmy got moving.

There was a steely glint in his eyes as he threaded his way through the groups beside the dance floor, slipping dexterously round a large dowager and dodging a red-faced, Poona-colonel type who, with a hiccough, asked him for a light for an already lit cigar. Nor did Jimmy heed the languorous redhead who turned her lovely back on her escort in order to bring the full battery of her inviting glance to bear on him as he went by.

One sentence the man had used to his companion at the buffet was ringing in his head like a warning bell: '*I saw him sneaking off with the judge to the billiard-room.*'

The billiard-room. And only a minute before the waiter had told the girl her father was waiting for her in the *library*. That he was taking a drink to him there.

And she'd followed the odd little man who looked so ill.

He gained the hall and gave a quick

look for Inspector Crow. He couldn't see him, but another figure whom he recognized hurried towards him.

'Would you be looking for someone. Mr. Strange?' Sergeant Warburton asked primly.

'Where's Crow?'

'The Inspector has retired momentarily in order to — er — wash his hands.'

'He'll be retired *permanently* if you don't find him quick!'

'What's happened?'

'Nothing — yet. Where's the library?'

The other indicated the other end of the hall. 'Turn to the right, along the passage, door facing you.'

'You find Crow and get to the billiard-room pronto. If Mr. Justice Henderson's there beat it like hell to the library. Savvy? Then make it snappy.'

Warburton hurried off.

Jimmy, his jaw set, reached the passage and in a moment was turning the handle of the library door. The door didn't budge. It was locked. A glance told him it would require more than his weight to burst it open. As he turned away he caught the muffled voices of the girl and the waiter within. Swiftly, purposefully, he went back towards the hall.

★ ★ ★

When Margot Henderson had followed the little man into the library he held the door open. She heard it shut after her as, with a little frown, she turned and said: 'I thought my father was here?'

It was then she saw the waiter turning the key.

'What are you doing? How dare you lock the door!'

When he faced her there was an ugly-looking automatic in his hand. His eyes were blazing and his voice sent a chill down her spine.

'Stay where you are. Don't make a sound.'

He's a madman, she thought, and realized her only chance was to keep cool and play for time. She spoke to him as if he were a wilful child. 'Put that gun away and let me out at once.'

He advanced towards her, the revolver

threatening her unwaveringly.

'All in good time,' he said.

As the menacing figure came closer her nerve snapped.

'You must be mad!' she gasped involuntarily, and drew back.

'And if I am, who's to blame?' He was trembling, the knuckles that gripped the automatic showed white. 'Mr. Justice Henderson! That's who's to blame — ' His voice rose hysterically. 'Mr. Justice Henderson, who sent my boy to the gallows!'

She backed away. Silently prayed her father or someone would arrive in time. For one heart-stopping moment she thought she heard the door-handle turn. The man before her appeared not to have noticed anything and she dare not cry out in case it made him shoot.

'I swore I'd get my own back,' he was babbling. 'Make him suffer the way he'd made me — '

'Who are you? What are you talking about?'

'I'm James Benson's father. And I'm talking about my son — or perhaps that doesn't mean anything to you?'

At the impact of his words the room spun dizzily before her for a moment. Then that's what the warning letter had been getting at.

Benson. The murderer her father had sentenced to death. And now *his* father . . . She made a tremendous effort to pull herself together. What could she say, what could she do that would keep his finger from pressing the trigger?

'Your father took my son from me,' he was raving, his face contorted with anguish and insane revenge. 'Now it's my turn to take you from him!'

'No, no!'

'And by God I'm going to do it!'

He lurched forward, the automatic thrust before him, and she closed her eyes.

As if from a great distance she heard a voice say:

'Reach for it, Benson. Move an inch and I'll blow you to hell and back!'

She opened her eyes just in time to see Benson turn his head and run his chin slap into a terrific punch unleashed by

Jimmy Strange. The waiter took no further interest in the proceedings.

'Pardon me popping in through the window,' Jimmy grinned at her, and she saw a curtain still stirring behind him, 'but the door was locked.' He crossed to her. 'You all right?'

She nodded breathlessly. 'Thank — thank heaven you came!' Pointing to the figure crumpled on the floor and a trifle hysterically: 'He — he was going to kill me!'

He flipped open his cigarette case.

'Nothing like a cigarette when you're scared stiff,' he said steadily. 'I always use one.'

She took one, smiling shakily at him. He lit it, then his own. He bent and pocketed the revolver which the other had dropped as he collapsed.

'His own fault I socked him so hard,' he said, almost apologetically. 'I told him not to move — '

'Where's your gun?'

He grinned at her amiably. 'Merely my somewhat vivid imagination. Comes in handy sometimes.'

'You seem to have the knack of coming

in handy yourself quite a lot!' And her eyes, looking into his, were very bright.

It was moments such as these of which he was wont to take appropriate advantage. But the idea was hit on the head by a vigorous rattling of the door-handle and an imperative bellowing noise without.

'That,' said Jimmy with a regretful sigh, 'would doubtless be Inspector Crow.'

She stared at him in wonderment. 'The police? But how . . . ?'

'I'll explain everything later,' he said, 'while we're dancing.' And he moved to the door and opened it.

The Inspector lumbered into the room, accompanied by an anxious-looking Mr. Justice Henderson, who rushed over to his daughter to enfold her in a thankful embrace. In the background hovered Sergeant Warburton.

'What the devil's been going on?' growled Crow.

Jimmy nodded towards the girl.

'Miss Henderson'll spill it, and — if you ask her very nicely — use only one-syllable words even you'll understand.'

The other's complexion turned a mottled hue and he began to utter curious sounds that threatened to interfere with his breathing.

'No, no,' Jimmy said quickly in mock protest, 'you mustn't praise my modesty! I did nothing, really. And now, if you'll forgive my retiring disposition . . . ' At the door he turned to the now almost apoplectic Crow and grinned: 'Besides, I've got one hell of a thirst.' And was gone.

A roar like that of a bull stung by some outsize wasp followed him.

It was the Inspector exploding his accumulated wrath upon the inoffensive and innocent Sergeant Warburton.

★　★　★

When, some time later, he was telling Sandra all about it, Jimmy was careful, of course, not to dwell on the good time he'd had. Dancing with the girl, for instance. He skipped that. Which was ever the way of Jimmy Strange in such matters.

Not that Sandra wasn't capable of filling in the bits he left out, anyway. She knew what Margot Henderson looked like, and she knew her Jimmy Strange. She let it go, though. Just gave him one of her sidelong speculative glances that made him grin a little uneasily, and let it go. Which was the way of Sandra in such matters — sometimes.

She said: 'When did you first catch on to the waiter?'

'Face was vaguely familiar the moment I saw him. But I couldn't quite fix him. It was the shock I got overhearing those two at the buffet clicked everything into place. Then I remembered I'd seen him at Bensoni's that day we lunched there.'

'I seem to remember a harassed little man hovering round the fat Italian woman who ran the place,'

'His wife,' she said. 'It was she wrote to the girl and the police.'

Through a puff of cigarette smoke he said: 'I knew that when the girl showed me the letter.'

She looked at him.

'That was extremely bright of you,' she

said. 'Or are you kidding?'

He said: 'Don't you remember you remarked about the funny way the menu was written out?'

'All twirls and twiddley bits, you mean?'

'Same in the letter. Couldn't miss it.'

'Bensoni — Benson,' she was murmuring.

'Imagine me never connecting the names until afterwards.'

She patted his hand. 'I think you did very nicely,' she said.

'And I'm sure Miss Henderson must have been terribly grateful.'

He caught the look she was giving him and grinned at her. Then adroitly changing the subject he glanced at his watch and said:

'Which reminds me — what about lunch now?' And taking her arm added in her ear; 'Somewhere extra special, darling, because from where I stand you look extra special today.'

'From where I stand,' she said, 'you look somewhat fascinating yourself. In fact, just the same lying, unprintable rogue as ever!'

And they went out laughing.

3

The Jealous Husband

Geoffrey Lane glanced impatiently at the cream-coloured telephone by his bedside. Jabbing a cigarette in his mouth with a nervously irritable gesture, he lit it and paced the room. As though to be free of the frustrating confines of the elegant gilt-panelled wall he flung open the french windows and stepped out on to the little balcony.

Below him the wide and spacious promenade of Westbourne lay, bathed in the golden haze of the summer's evening, and beyond it the yellow sands ran down to a smooth, glimmering sea. But the beauty of the panorama made little appeal to the man who scowled down at it from his room at the Hotel Majestic, that luxurious cream and gold caravanserai of one of the South Coast's most fashionable resorts.

Geoffrey Lane pulled at his evening tie and turned back into the room. As he did so the telephone jangled into life. With a muttered exclamation of relief, he crossed quickly and lifted the receiver. The woman's voice over the wire smoothed the scowl from his face, drove the tension from the lines round his mouth.

'Geoffrey, darling! I couldn't ring you earlier — '

'What happened? Where are you?'

'Here — at the hotel, of course.'

'The number of your room, what is it?'

'I'm on the floor above you.'

'The number, quickly!'

There was a smile in her voice as she answered him slowly, conscious of the power she exercised over him.

'Two-o-one . . . if you must know.'

'I'm coming up — '

'No, no, you can't do that.'

'I must see you. Oh, my darling, you can't imagine how long it's been, this waiting — '

'I know, my dear, but please — '

'What is it?'

'It — it's too risky.'

'Nonsense! You're trying to put me off. What is it? What's wrong? You agreed to come down here, and now . . . ' He spoke quickly, harshly.

'It's too risky, I tell you,' she said, her voice level and cool. 'He's followed me. I've seen him.'

'What! You mean he's here?'

He puffed ineffectually at his cigarette, which had gone out.

'He's here,' she said.

'But when did he arrive? How did he know?'

'He was here a few minutes ago. He's just gone down to have a drink.'

With a vicious gesture of frustration, he crushed the cold cigarette into the ashtray by the telephone. For a moment he babbled incoherently into the mouthpiece, ill concealing his chagrin and bitter dismay. 'But I *must* see you — I must! Can't I come up to your room for a moment?'

'I daren't let you. I'm frightened . . . '

'Don't be so silly — he won't be coming back yet.'

'It — it's not silly. Geoffrey, I think he suspects.'

'Suspects? How d'you mean?'

'Why, that you and I — '

'Oh, rubbish, my dear! How could he think that I . . . ?'

'Well, I'm sure he knows something. What made him change his mind at the last minute and come down here?'

'Just coincidence, that's all. How could it be anything else?'

'He's been acting so oddly.'

'Be sensible, darling. Please let me — '

He broke off and turned as the door behind him opened slowly.

His eyes widened in amazement as he saw her husband standing there.

The woman at the other end was speaking again as he fumbled to replace the receiver and let it fall with a sharp clatter on to the table.

'Marsden!' he gulped.

And then as the other came forward to reveal an automatic held menacingly pointed at him, Lane's voice rose in a croak of fear. 'Good God, man, what — '

'Shut up!' Marsden said, through lips that were a grim line. With his heel he shut the door behind him. He went on, his tone cold and expressionless: 'You needn't put your hands up, Lane. It won't make the slightest difference.'

'Now listen, Marsden. I don't know what — '

The man behind the evil-looking revolver ignored his attempt to speak. He said coolly: 'Surprised, aren't you? Thought I was well out of the way. That I didn't know about you and Helen — '

Lane made a tremendous effort to gain control of the situation. Perspiration glistened on his face and he trembled as he stepped forward purposefully.

'Don't be a damn fool,' he said heavily. 'Put down that gun.'

'You dirty rat,' the other went on evenly. 'I've been watching you. Watching you for a long time — and now you're going to — '

Lane was moving towards him as the gun barked. For a moment he stood, swaying slightly, staring at Marsden through the little cloud of acrid smoke. Then his face contorted in agony and he dropped to the floor. As he fell he knocked over a table lamp.

There came a metallic scream from the telephone receiver that lay where it had fallen alongside its cream cradle beside the bed. Then came a distorted babble of words. Then the line went dead. On the floor above a door slammed.

★　★　★

Jimmy Strange was leisurely tying his black tie when he heard the revolver-shot. He paused for a moment, one eyebrow raised quizzically. Then, observing that his tie was still slightly crooked, he pulled it into shape. He stood back from the mirror, flicked a purely imaginary speck of dust from the lapel of his immaculate dinner jacket, lit a cigarette and strolled out of the room.

The reason for Jimmy Strange's not undistinguished presence at the Hotel Majestic that weekend could be described in one word of magical significance. Sandra. Do not let this reason, amply sufficient as it may appear, occasion the faintest lift of an interrogatory eyebrow, however. For — perhaps, oddly enough

— Sandra was not a weekend guest at the hotel. That delectable piece of alluring femininity was, in fact, many miles away at that moment, in London.

Nevertheless, she was still the reason why Jimmy had come down that evening to Westbourne. He had run away from her. Put more plainly, he was escaping from the risk that he might ask Sandra to marry him. And be accepted. That was the only fault he had to find with her since the day almost of their first meeting. She was so attractive, so desirable, that there were far too many other guys around ready, eager and willing to step into his shoes with alacrity. And, moreover, any one of them would, in order to reserve her for himself alone and forever, up and marry her like a shot.

Now Sandra, in spite of a figure that was a dream of delight and a face that was a delightful dream, was a nice girl. She wanted to get married. To the right man. And Jimmy, to whom she'd made it pretty plain that he was the right man, was becoming increasingly aware that it was about time he put the all-important question. And that if left too late he'd wake up one morning to find himself at her wedding — as best man, wearing a rueful smile.

All the same, the prospect of losing her was grimly depressing. Thus, making suitable excuses, he'd slipped away for a quiet weekend, deliberately to avoid her dangerous proximity that might cause him to ask that question he knew he would afterwards inevitably regret. The brief break would, he felt, give him a chance to take a grip on himself and he'd return complete with his old level-headed equanimity.

Now stepping into the corridor to investigate the origin of the revolver-shot, he grinned to himself. Perhaps it wasn't going to be the quiet weekend he'd anticipated, after all!

His grin widened as he saw a few rooms away a woman beating her hands against a door.

'Let me in!' she was sobbing. 'Open the door — oh, please let me in!'

Jimmy puffed out a cloud of cigarette smoke, and his eyes narrowed, unobtrusively approached her. He noted that she was wearing a revealingly modelled evening gown and that jewellery flashed from the hands that continued to beat on the door.

'Open the door!' Her voice rose hysterically. 'You *must* open it!'

She was unaware of him until he stood close to her and said:

'What goes on?'

With a sobbing gasp she turned, and he was pleasurably intrigued to observe that she was decidedly attractive. Sleek, dark hair, wide, slightly slanted eyes. She spelt sophisticated allure in capital letters. He sensed that she spelt something else, too. In even bigger letters. Danger. With that warning signal ringing somewhere back of his brain, Jimmy tapped the ash off his cigarette and waited for her to recover from the surprise of his presence at her side.

'I'm afraid I startled you,' he said reassuringly.

'Oh!' she gasped. 'Something — something dreadful's happened!'

'Anything I can do to help?'

She stared at him piteously. 'I don't

know. My husband's in there, and I must get in — '

'You mean he's locked you out?'

'No, no — it — it's someone else's room. But he's there I know. I could hear him over the 'phone — and the shot.'

'The shot?'

Jimmy Strange's eyes regarded her shrewdly. She was terrified about something all right. From her few gabbled words he'd pieced together part of what had happened. The fact that she was outside 'someone else's' room, with her husband on the inside, told him plenty.

She was saying, the words half choked by her fear:

'I ran downstairs. Oh, this is terrible! He's shot him — my husband's shot him!'

'Shot who?'

'Geoffrey.'

Jimmy nodded. He had the angle — or rather the triangle — on it. She was just the sort, he decided, who'd never be satisfied with only one man around. Even the man she'd married. She craved the flattery, the sordid excitement of other men's company. And it looked as if this time she'd got some poor fool, and herself, into a jam.

She was beating at the door again.

'Oh, let me in! *Let me in!*'

Jimmy was turning over in his mind whether he should offer to try one of his parlour-tricks on the lock and open the door for her, when there came the scrape of the key on the inside.

'Thank God!' the woman breathed, and stood back, relief and apprehension mingled in her expression.

The door opened, and a man in evening dress stood there. The woman gave a gasp of surprise.

'*Geoffrey*! But I thought you were . . . Where's Charles?'

Geoffrey Lane surveyed her calmly, though Jimmy noted that a little nerve was twitching beneath his left eye.

'Your husband?' the man queried, in apparent puzzlement. 'I don't know. He's not here.'

She stared at him, bewildered.

'But I — I heard him. He — '

'My dear,' he interrupted her firmly,

with an oblique glance at Jimmy, 'pull yourself together . . . Come in and have a drink.' He looked questioningly at Jimmy, as if aware for the first time of his presence. He said: 'Is this gentleman with you?'

The tip of Jimmy's tongue touched his lips in anticipation of receiving an invitation to join in the offered refreshment — but the expression on the other's somewhat set features was not encouraging. Hiding his disappointment, he said airily:

'Oh, don't mind me. I — er — just happened to come out of my room when I thought I heard a shot.'

The man glanced quickly at him, then at the woman. There was a moment's silence, then: 'Yes, it did sound like one.' Geoffrey Lane's expression contrived to relax until it appeared almost affable. 'But it must have been a car, I think.'

And with a nod of dismissal, he turned to the woman.

'Come along, Helen.' Over his shoulder he called: 'Goodbye.'

Jimmy stared at the closed door

through a cloud of cigarette smoke. He turned on his heel and made his way back to his own room, a thoughtful frown shadowing his face.

He stood before his mirror and automatically straightened his tie, while he pondered over the little scene he had witnessed.

'Odd. Definitely odd,' he mused. 'Car my ruddy elbow! That bang was an *automatic*, or my name's not James but Jasmine . . . ' He scowled at his reflection. 'And then what the woman said suggested that while she'd been chin wagging over the blower with dear Geoffrey, who was in his room below, she'd heard hubby come in and take a pot at him . . . Then what a hell of a time he'd been opening his door to her, with her trying to break it down with her bare hands . . . Oh, odd, Jimmy, my lad, and fairly asking to be looked into!'

He lit a fresh cigarette.

'It would be vaguely interesting to know, also,' he continued, musingly, 'what's happened to hubby. It was *him* she expected to be in the bedroom, bumping off her boyfriend . . . '

Glancing at the window, his mouth suddenly quirked at the corners with a grin. He crossed and looked down for a moment at the promenade and the sea, over which the gloom of approaching night was now falling. He opened the french windows and stepped on to the narrow balcony.

Moving like a shadow and ducking behind the balcony railing so that he would not be observed from below, he made his way swiftly across to the balcony of the room adjoining his. It appeared to be unoccupied, and he had passed it and stood outside the french windows of the room beyond. It was this room, he calculated, wherein the man called Geoffrey was now knocking back a drink with the wife of another man.

His ear close to the window he could hear her speaking:

'I knew it was him. I was sure I couldn't have mistaken Charles' voice.'

The man replied:

'The fool! Trying to shoot me like that. Luckily, he missed — '

'Thank God!'

'I pretended he'd hit me. I flopped down and he must have panicked. He rushed out on to the balcony and got away through the room next door. Fortunately it's empty. Then I heard you at the door.'

'I thought he'd killed you!'

'Damned near did!' growled the other. 'Shook me up, I can tell you. I thought it'd be as well to make sure he'd pushed off before I opened the door to you.'

'That was why you were so long?'

'I thought it would be safer for you. But he'd gone all right.'

'Oughtn't we to find him?'

'No need to worry about that for the moment.'

'But, Geoffrey — '

'He left me for dead and he'll make himself scarce. For his own sake, we've got to keep this business quiet.'

'Of course.'

'Have another drink, darling? You look a bit white still.'

There was the sound of drinks being mixed. Jimmy thought longingly of what he could do to a double Scotch and cautiously eased his cramped position. After a moment, he heard the wife say:

'You're sure he got into the room next door all right, Geoffrey? It's getting dark and he might have slipped on the balcony, and — '

'Rubbish! I tell you he's got away scot-free.' His tone took on an aggrieved tone. 'Why you should be worrying about him, when *I've* been nearly murdered by the blighter — '

'It's not that, darling,' she said quickly, mollifying him. 'But if anything has happened to him, there'd be the dickens of a commotion. People asking questions — '

'Oh, pull yourself together,' the other snapped. 'Charles is all right. If you don't believe me, climb out on to the balcony and see for yourself.'

Jimmy drew in his breath sharply and flattened himself against the wall, still crouched down, as he heard the woman approach the windows. As she manipulated the bolt that held one window shut, he considered the chances of making a

101

dash back to his own room. He decided he couldn't possibly make it without being spotted. All he could do was to make himself look as much like a stray cat as possible — without much hope of success!

Then, just as he was racking his brain for a plausible answer to the inevitable questions that would follow his discovery, and had decided that the excuse of sleep-walking wouldn't cut any ice, he heard her say;

'Oh, I can't shift this bolt — I expect you're right, Charles is safe enough.'

There was a muttered agreement from the man and Jimmy breathed freely again as the woman moved away from the window.

The other was asking, his voice rising sharply:

'By the way, Helen, who was that chap outside the door?'

'Never seen him before,' was the reply. 'He just appeared on the scene out of the blue.'

'Hmm . . . Well, I choked him off all right, and he won't bother us again.'

102

There followed a slight pause, then in more casual tones the man went on: 'You know, I think it'd be better if I got back to London tonight.'

'Geoffrey! Why?'

'Well, I — '

'You're not going to leave me here, by myself — '

'Darling, please do calm yourself . . . Don't you see — your husband may turn up again, and it'd be better if I'm not here. Surely, that's commonsense?'

'I suppose you're right,' she agreed doubtfully.

'Now, you run along and fix your make-up,' he suggested amiably, 'you've been crying a little, poor pet — and I'll meet you downstairs.'

'You think we should risk having dinner together?' There might have been a hint of sarcasm in her voice.

He laughed shortly.

'I think we can. Anyway, I'd rather die with a full stomach!'

'Don't joke about it, Geoffrey, please.'

Followed some murmured endearments from the man, then the woman went out.

Jimmy was about to make a move back to his room, having decided that he'd heard all there was to hear, when he caught the sound of the man flashing his telephone. He waited and listened again. The man was saying:

'Give me Reception, please ... Reception? Oh, I shall be leaving tonight ... ' There followed some words that Jimmy couldn't catch. Then: 'Yes, the eleven-twenty for London. Will you arrange about my luggage and a taxi ... ? Only a suitcase and a trunk ... Yes, better be here at eleven sharp ... '

A few minutes later Jimmy Strange strolled across the hotel foyer towards the reception clerk. Men and women in evening dress brushed past him; a waiter, his expression anxiously purposeful, whisked by; a pretty girl, gazing around for her escort, paused to give him a veiled glance that was not without interest, but — for once — Jimmy was oblivious of her passing, only his nostrils quivered at the cloud of exotic perfume that trailed after her. But his mind was on other things. He was intent only on a certain piece of information he was seeking. One or two details he needed in order to fill in more completely the picture of the drama he had butted into upstairs.

Casually he said to the desk clerk:

'Wonder if I might have a glimpse of your visitors' book?'

'Certainly, sir.'

'Chap I saw leaving room one-fourteen just now — I know his face, but can't quite place him,' Jimmy said as he pulled the heavy book towards him.

'Often the way, sir,' the clerk smiled understandingly.

Jimmy ran a finger down the column of names.

'Let's see . . . Ah, here we are! Room one-fourteen. Geoffrey Lane. London. Nationality, British. That's the chap all right.

'Is that the gentleman you have in mind, sir?'

'Yes, thanks. Has he been here long?'

'Mr. Lane, sir? Matter of three weeks.'

Jimmy nodded and moved towards the dining room, whence dance music was being rhythmically dispensed. Not at all displeased with the information he had obtained, humming to the tune that was being played, he strolled down the wide, short stairway into the room.

The *maitre d'hôtel* hurried obsequiously forward and led him to his table. A waiter bowed over him with the menu.

'Large Scotch-and-soda,' Jimmy murmured mechanically as the inevitable prelude to his order.

'Yessair.'

He concluded his order and glancing round, observed:

'Quite a crowd tonight.'

'It is always the same weekends, sair.'

'Tell me . . . would that be Mrs. Lane dancing with Mr. Lane over there?'

'Er — Mrs. Lane? No, sair. That is Mrs. Marsden.'

'Oh, my mistake.'

The waiter bent lower to add with an almost imperceptible cough:

'I have not seen Mr. Marsden, sair. I do not think he comes here.'

Jimmy grinned and said: 'Quite!'

The waiter bowed and swept away.

Presently, when he was sure that Lane and Mrs. Marsden were engrossed with the fish course and each other's conversation, Jimmy drained his whisky and unobtrusively quitted the dining room.

He found the first floor deserted. He stood outside room one-fourteen and with a glance up and down began his adroit manipulation with the lock. A few moments later he was knowledgeably inspecting another lock of a cabin-trunk inside room one-fourteen. Again he proceeded to perform something that was slightly more skilful than a mere parlour trick. The trunk was open. Its contents tightened his mouth into a grim line, brought a chill light to his narrowed eyes.

'So *that's* your bright idea, Mr. Geoffrey Lane!' he mused. He closed the trunk again. Snapped back the lock — and then wheeled round, tensed for action.

Someone was turning a key in the door.

For a second he thought of making a dash for it via the window.

But with the realization that it was too

late came a better notion. He threw himself on to the bed, quickly disarranged his hair and sprawled back with an inane grin.

Geoffrey Lane came in to stare at him in angry amazement.

From his look of surprised recognition, Jimmy guessed that the other's unexpected return was connected with some relatively trivial errand, such as a forgotten cigarette case or handkerchief, and not to do with him. At this rapid deduction, Jimmy gave a mental sigh of relief. He might get out of the spot yet.

''Lo, ol' man,' he greeted him tipsily. 'C'mon in!'

'You again! What the hell are you doing here?'

Jimmy giggled, tried to raise himself on his elbow, and flopped back again. Lane gave a glance at the trunk, then at him, suspicion sharpening his look. 'What are you doing in my room?' he rasped.

Making what seemed to be a tremendous effort, Jimmy sat up, eyeing the other blearily. '*Your* room, ol' man?' he queried thickly.

He giggled again, interrupting it with an artistically simulated hiccough. 'Don' be shilly!'

Lane advanced upon him threateningly. 'I shan't ask you again,' he glowered. '*What are you doing here?*'

'Sssshush!' Jimmy raised an admonishing finger, and then smoothed the pillow. 'You'll wake the baby!' He lurched to his feet, swaying. 'Have a drink? Oh! 'S'funny, whersh the bottle? 'S'disappeared! M'glash's disappeared, too!' He giggled again, and half supporting himself on the other's shoulder, spoke in a whisper that betokened a world-shattering revelation. 'D'you know, ol' man — d'you know what? I believe we're in the wrong room!'

Lane shook him off angrily, but the suspicion receded from his face. 'Drunken fool!' he exclaimed.

Jimmy giggled again. 'He-he! Let'sh see what's the number of thish room.' He reeled to the door, opened it and staggered back into the room. 'Two hunn'red 'n' fourteen,' he announced, blinking owlishly. 'What did I tell you? *My* room's two hunn'red 'n' twenty. Proves it.'

'That still doesn't explain how you got in here.'

'I rememmer now. I went to ask the liftboy to get 'nother bottle, 'n' I mush've got in here by' — another hiccough — 'mish-take.'

'This door was *locked*,' cut in Lane chillingly.

Jimmy hiccoughed once more to give himself time in which to think up the answer to that one. He grinned again and said:

'Thash what you think, ol' man.'

'What d'you mean?'

''Cos when I was coming in, the cham'er-maid was coming out. See?'

The other made no reply, but seemed to accept the explanation with some relief. He threw another furtive, quick glance at the trunk as Jimmy sidled drunkenly to the door.

'Well, I s'pose I'd better toddle off to my own li'l nest — '

Lane helped him out of the room with an unceremonious shove. 'Come on! Get out!'

Jimmy allowed himself to be hustled into the corridor, protesting loudly. 'All ri', ol' man, all ri'! Whash the hurry?'

The door slammed on him. And with a muttered: 'Oh, what a rude man!' he tottered along to his room.

Some time later found Jimmy chatting to the commissionaire at the hotel entrance:

'Where d'you get your taxis?'

'Off the station rank, sir — always rely on them. Will you be wanting one, sir?'

'Not just now. I was just — er — wondering, that's all.'

And with a little smile flickering across his lips he went in search of a telephone. As he shut himself in one of the hotel callboxes the smile on his face grew wider. He picked up the receiver.

★ ★ ★

In his office at Scotland Yard, Inspector Crow scowled at the clock on his desk and heaved himself to his feet. It was late and he'd had a heavy day. Reaching for his bowler, he mentally savoured the steak-and-kidney pudding, which his loving and dutiful wife would be keeping warm for him. But his gastronomical anticipations were to be shattered by the sudden appearance of Sergeant Warburton at the door. The Sergeant was bearing a slip of paper and his lips were in a prim line.

'Could anything be more vexatious, sir?' he murmured querulously in answer to his superior's brusque inquiry.

'What *is* it?' growled Crow with heavy patience.

'It's a message from that wretched Strange person.'

The Inspector banged his hat on his desk with a thud.

'Gawdalmighty!' he roared. 'Can't that ruddy nuisance let me clock off in peace sometimes?' The other made a commiserating noise, and Crow turned on him wrathfully. 'Well, don't stand there like a pantomime fairy! What is it?'

Sergeant Warburton went pink. 'It's a message they took at the switchboard, sir. Apparently this Strange person didn't wish to speak to you personally.'

'Guilty conscience,' the Inspector grunted.

Warburton coughed delicately. 'Not exactly, sir, if I may contradict you. The reason he gave was that — er — the sound of your voice would ruin his dinner.'

Inspector Crow made no comment. He merely drew his ginger eyebrows together in a forbidding glare, muttering something to the effect that it would be he himself who'd be having his dinner ruined. The thought of having to miss that hot steak-and-kidney pie was unbearable. 'Read the message,' he grunted wearily.

Sergeant Warburton pouted.

'It — er — it's somewhat disrespectfully worded, sir — '

'*Read it!*'

'As you wish, sir.' He read:

'*Crow, Old Bird.*

How about a spot of ozone to pep up your appetite — plus a nice little murder all neatly tied up for you? Then come to Westbourne — it's so bracing! Be there — at the local police station — by eleven o'clock tonight, and you'll

113

click for a present from the seaside! It won't be a stick of rock, either. But then you aren't a sweet-tooth, are you, Old Sourpuss?

As ever, Jimmy Strange.'

Warburton's nose twitched in delicate disapproval as he concluded the message. 'Distinctly discourteous, sir, and, to my mind, doesn't make sense.'

Crow's expression was bitter. Through gritted teeth he growled: 'Plain enough to me that there's something up at Westbourne which Strange has ferreted out. We'd better get down there, and' — with a glance at the clock — 'if we want to make it by eleven, we'll have to move. Fast!'

'Tonight's the night I usually wash my hair, sir — ' began Sergeant Warburton tentatively.

'Hell-fire singe your blasted hair!' exploded Crow, the veins standing out on his forehead like cords. 'Get the car ready. *Move!*'

And Sergeant Warburton meekly but hurriedly withdrew.

The Hotel Majestic luggage porter and the man in taxi driver's cap grunted as they handled the trunk preparatory to hoisting it on to the waiting taxi.

'Cripes!' muttered the porter. 'Bit of a weight, eh?'

'Yus,' said the other, in a gin-and-fog croak.

'Must be full o' bricks!'

'Yus.'

'Rather heavy, I'm afraid,' said Geoffrey Lane from the taxi's interior.

'We'll manage it, sir,' said the porter, and to his companion, who was re-knotting his thick scarf more securely round his ears: 'Ready ter lift, mate?'

'Yus.'

'Then h'up she goes!'

And with much grunting and heavy breathing the trunk was safely deposited on the cab, and while the other clambered into the driver's seat, the porter slammed the door and touched his forehead expectantly. 'Thank you, sir.' He turned and instructed: 'Station, mate.'

'Yus.'

'Blimey! D'you always say 'yus', mate?'

'Yus.'

And the taxi drove off.

Several minutes later it pulled up, and the driver leant out, opened the door and extended his vocabulary to mutter hoarsely: ''Ere y'are sir.'

Geoffrey Lane got out — and saw the blue lamp jutting out from the wall overhead. With a quick indrawn gasp he turned on the other:

'You fool! This is the police station!'

'Yus,' was the inevitable monosyllabic response. But this time it was accompanied by an unexpectedly swift punch which draped itself neatly on Lane's jaw. As his passenger slumped quietly to the ground, the other loosened his scarf slightly and observed: 'That'll keep you quiet!'

He turned and squeezed the motor-horn loudly. In a moment a policeman appeared through the door beneath the lamp,

'Now then, now then! What's all this?'

'Inspector Crow there?'

'An' supposing he *is*?'

'Only that the present wot was promised 'im 'as arrived,' was the croaked reply.

The policeman's jaw dropped as he saw the figure the other was indicating lying inert on the pavement. The hoarse voice went on: 'Better fetch Inspector Crow, quick — and tell him ter take a look at the gent's luggage while 'e's abaht it!'

'Wait here, I'll get the Inspector . . . '

'Yus.'

In a moment, the policeman, his tones raised excitedly and with Inspector Crow behind him, reappeared. 'Taximan here says — ' He broke off and glanced up and down the street. 'Blimey! He's 'opped it!'

'Never mind about him,' grunted Crow, his heavy bottle jaw stuck out aggressively. 'Take care of this man here. Get him inside. He's out cold.'

The policeman called for assistance and the unconscious Geoffrey Lane was carried into the police station.

The Inspector eyed the trunk on the taxi calculatingly. He muttered to Sergeant Warburton, standing at his elbow; 'What was it the driver chap said about the luggage?'

'Something to the effect that you should look into it, sir,' volunteered the other pedantically.

'We'll start on this trunk. Come on, give me a hand.'

Together they wrestled it off the taxi, the Sergeant wearing an air of distaste at having to indulge in such manual labour, and Crow muttering ripe curses beneath his grampus-like breathing.

'Now,' he gasped, 'get a spanner — we'll crack the lock open and see what's inside. Come on, Sergeant!'

The lock soon yielded, and as they opened the trunk the Inspector grunted to Sergeant Warburton: 'Now, for Pete's sake, don't say you faint at the sight o' blood!'

★ ★ ★

'As you'll have no doubt guessed,' said Jimmy to Sandra over drinks two days later, 'when the pie was opened there was the body of Charles Marsden. Not a very dainty dish, I'm afraid, to set before anyone.'

Sandra shuddered and he took her hand.

'Not unnaturally, of course, this discovery somewhat upset Lane's getaway. In fact,' he went on, 'he finally confessed that Marsden had missed him with the shot the wife and I heard, and foxing him, he grabbed him from behind and strangled him.'

After a moment Sandra said:

'Not exactly a quiet weekend for you, darling.'

'It took my mind off things,' he grinned.

'Such as?'

He hesitated. Then: 'Oh . . . things, you know. Being away from you, and all that.'

Her glance was tender.

'I'm glad you missed me,' she said huskily.

Uneasily he realized he'd not had a moment, while he'd been away, to think up a plan whereby he could duck marrying Sandra but still at the same time not lose her. Been too busy, he told himself morosely, poking his nose into someone else's trouble to worry about his own. He still had *his* tricky problem to solve . . .

Sandra was saying:

'By the way, what happened to the taxi

driver? He seemed to be mixed up in it pretty well.'

'Yes, mysterious-like, wasn't he?' Then suddenly Jimmy spoke in a hoarse gin-and-fog croak: 'Shoved orf, 'e did, inter the night — modest sorter bloke.' And added the one inevitable monosyllable: 'Yus!'

Sandra laughed delightedly.

'Oh, Jimmy, you really are heavenly! If only I could've seen you in that borrowed get-up, driving that taxi!'

He joined in her amusement. He thought no woman could laugh so attractively as she did. Perhaps, after all, being married to her wouldn't be such a tie? She really was so lovely, so deliciously desirable. They'd have wonderful times together.

He leaned forward impulsively.

'Darling.'

'Yes. Jimmy?'

'Darling . . . ' and then grinned, as involuntarily it seemed his voice took on a gin-and-fog croak: 'Wot abaht another drink? Yus?'

4

The Forgiving Financier

The 'phone came to life, its burr-burr making him jump slightly. He paused and eyed it with a puzzled frown. It was the first time it had rung for several weeks and he had no reason to expect a call this morning. He got up from the letter he was writing, lifted the receiver. As he did so he decided it would be a wrong number anyway.

But the voice was familiar in his ear. Startlingly familiar.

'Alan Page?'

'Yes . . . ' He answered hesitantly, still unable to credit his hearing. It was over a year ago when he'd last heard that voice, and its vicious brutality, its vindictive malice on that occasion had not been easily forgotten. Now the voice was soft, charged with warmth and friendliness.

'You're surprised to hear from me, no doubt?'

'It is a bit unexpected, I must admit' — with a little laugh of embarrassment.

'I want us to be friends again, my boy.'

He made no reply, there was nothing he could think of to say. He could only frown in puzzlement and wonder if he was dreaming. Or if the other was dreaming, talking in his sleep, or something. The voice in his ear went on, after a cough of hesitation — that characteristic clearing of the throat that took Page back to the library, with the sun streaming through the french windows, and the expensive aroma of after-breakfast cigar as the man who at this moment was talking to him over the wire dictated the morning's correspondence to him. He presumed the other was speaking from the library now.

'I want to let bygones be bygones. I realize I behaved harshly towards you, allowed my emotions to get the better of me. I should have accepted the situation, been more understanding, retained my sense of humour, shall we say? I ask you to believe how much — how very deeply — I regret what happened.'

'Why, yes — of course — '

'You think we can bury the hatchet?'

'I don't see why not. I mean — well — I — '

'You are being very generous, my boy. Magnanimous.'

'Not at all,' Again he gave an embarrassed little laugh. This was a side of the other man's character, which, despite his long acquaintance with him, he had never known existed. It fairly took the wind out of his sails. Again that familiar clearing of the throat in his ear.

'I — er — I understand Nadia is in New York?'

'Yes. That's right. She's in New York.'

'And you — er — you are both happy?'

'Well, it's not much fun being so far away from each other — '

'Quite. Of course, of course.' His tone was deeply sympathetic.

Page glanced at the letter he was writing. Gave an involuntary half-smile as he thought of the extra news he'd have to tell her. How astonished she'd be. Nadia wouldn't believe it, she'd accuse him of fooling. He said:

'But I'm hoping to be able to join her there very soon.'

'Good.' There was a short silence. Then: 'I'm giving a party tomorrow night, that's my excuse for 'phoning you, as a matter of fact. I — er — will you come?'

'Oh.'

'Thought we might have a drink and shake hands. See if there is anything I could do to make up for — for what happened. What d'you say, Page?'

'It's very kind of you.'

'It is you who'll be doing me a kindness. You'll accept then? Splendid. I shall look forward to seeing you.'

He didn't want to go in the slightest. He had no wish to see him again. Not that he felt any bitterness towards him. It was just that he didn't want to have anything to do with him any more. He knew he would only be embarrassed by the meeting. Nadia wouldn't want it, either. All the same, he couldn't think up any excuse that wouldn't sound as if he was still carrying a chip on his shoulder.

He hadn't courage, somehow, to slam the door on the proffered handshake, the persuasively friendly invitation to forget a past unpleasantness.

He sat over the letter for some time afterwards, his face still puzzled, troubled even, before he eventually gave a shrug and began writing where he'd left off when the 'phone had interrupted him.

★ ★ ★

Inspector Crow stared at the piece of paper before him with such concentrative power, his massive chin and jutting brows seemed as if they might meet. Apparently, however, what he saw caused him a certain amount of interest, for he gave a grunt and without removing his fixed regard felt, with a great hand, for his pipe sheltering coyly beneath the documents and files on his desk. He found it, pushed it thoughtfully into his face, produced a box of matches and lit the charred bowl, singeing one ginger eyebrow in the process. This slight mishap passed unnoticed, even the aroma of burning bristle blended un-remarked with the acrid odour from his pipe.

He gave another grunt and again the mighty fist reached out, this time to a drawer at his knee. Producing a magnifying glass, he brought it to bear upon the paper and squinted through it, his features contorted as if the effort was unbearable. Several moments passed, the silence of the office broken only by the Inspector's stertorous breathing and the curious bubbling noises emanating from his pipe.

Again a grunt, once more the hand reached out, one thick finger to search for and press heavily upon the bell-button. In quick response to his summons came a knock on the door, and Sergeant Warburton entered, to recoil for a second, as was his habit, at the smell of smouldering old rope that hung like a fogbank over his superior officer. Recovering himself, he advanced, permitting himself a discreet choking spasm as the tobacco fumes clogged his windpipe. With an air of resignation upon his prim features, Warburton stood waiting patiently for the other to speak.

Crow, who hadn't raised his eyes, seemed unaware of his presence. The Sergeant choked apologetically again, and the Inspector, his eyes still riveted to the piece of paper, muttered:

'Pity you don't take that cough out and drown it some time.'

The other compressed his lips and made no reply. After a moment Crow leaned back, put down the magnifying glass and said: 'Financial newspapers.'

Warburton, who had been admiring the sinuous patterns made by the tobacco smoke swirling against the ceiling, looked slightly startled.

'Financial newspapers,' repeated the Inspector, his voice rising. Sergeant Warburton blushed in confusion, and for a fleeting second considered the possibility of the other having suddenly gone mad and imagining himself to be a high-powered financier or Stock Exchange big-shot. As Crow was now roaring at him quite normally, however, he rapidly rejected the idea and made an attempt to understand what, he gathered, were some sort of instructions.

'Don't stand there like a ruddy palm tree,' the Inspector was exploding. 'Get out and buy me the financial newspapers. All of 'em.'

Light broke upon Warburton, though somewhat mistily, and he beat a retreat. As the door closed behind him, Inspector Crow's bellow rang inevitably in his ears:

'And I'd like 'em *today!*'

The Sergeant was back in remarkably short time, bearing an armful of the required journals, which he deposited on Crow's desk. The latter grabbed a couple immediately from the bundle and his eyes glinted as if there was something especially outstanding about these particular two. Warburton noticed they were the *Financial Market* and the *Investor's News*. He watched, with uncomprehending interest, as the Inspector bent over them, apparently comparing first one then the other, with the bit of paper before him. Finally, with a muttered exclamation, he seemed to find what he sought and choosing the second newspaper marked off a portion of one column heavily in pencil. He next proceeded to squint at the pencilled paragraphs through his magnifying glass, then at the piece of paper, and back again, his pipe bubbling and gurgling as if with excitement.

At length he appeared satisfied with the result of his examination and pushed back his chair to notice Warburton standing beside the desk. 'Oh, you're there,' he glowered at him.

'Yes, sir.'

Crow grunted, then handed the other the small bit of paper. Sergeant Warburton gazed at it carefully, observed it had been torn from an ordinary writing pad and on it were gummed letters obviously cut from a newspaper or magazine. The letters formed the following message:

Dear Sir — someone will be after the crimson lake tonight. This is a warning from a well-wisher.

It didn't mean a great deal to the Sergeant, but he tried to convey by his expression that it was of the deepest significance. Fortunately he was aided in this not unnaturally difficult performance by the Inspector's somewhat enlightening observation:

'Crimson Lake's a ruby owned by Curtis Sutcliffe, the financier. Valuable jewel.' He nodded towards the message. 'Sutcliffe received that this morning. Brought it along for me to look unto.'

'Oh, I see, sir,' Warburton nodded sagely. 'What it must be like to possess such Croesus-like wealth,' he said irrelevantly.

Crow threw him an impatient scowl and muttered: 'What in hell are you burbling about?'

The other abandoned his wishful-thinking and said quickly: 'Had he any suspicion as to the identity of the sender?'

'Nobody in particular. But he's giving a big party tonight and pointed out there'll be two or three hundred guests — '

'Among whom may well be one whose predilection for precious stones amounts to criminal proportions?' Sergeant War-burton put in with animation.

The Inspector eyed him sourly. 'I wish you wouldn't butt in,' he growled. 'All that long-winded drip makes my ruddy head reel.'

Warburton blushed apologetically, and Crow added: 'That's what he is afraid of.'

'Personally, 1 would suggest, sir,' Warburton ventured, 'that if he put the ruby safely under lock and key somewhere he would have no cause for anxiety.'

The Inspector's eyes rolled upwards as if calling upon a higher power to witness his long-suffering patience. Then he glared at the Sergeant, whose pedantic verbosity had ceased abruptly. 'Will you go and smother yourself,' he grated viciously. He stabbed at the marked newspaper with a thick finger. 'Why d'you think *I* have been brooding over this? To lay an egg?' He went on with a snort; 'But since you're so blasted smart, perhaps you'll tell me what you make of it all.'

He pushed the newspaper, which was of a pinkish shade, at Sergeant Warburton, together with the magnifying glass. The Sergeant applied it to the pencilled column. All he could glean was that it was an extract from some company report, riddled with technical terms and references. Had it been written in Aztec it

131

couldn't have told him less.

'Most interesting,' he murmured hopefully.

'Now this,' Crow rasped, handing him the anonymous message.

The other stared at the letters through the glass and realized, almost at once, what it was his superior had got so excited about. The letters forming the message had obviously been cut out from an issue of the financial sheet he'd just been examining. Comparison proved that the type was identical with that of the pencil-marked column. Under the magnifying glass he observed a pinkish edge he hadn't noticed before round each letter so neatly gummed to the writing paper, which was the exact shade of the newspaper.

Crow saw by the other's face that the idea had sunk in. 'Came a great light,' he grunted with heavy sarcasm. He continued: 'And if you can keep that trap of yours shut for a minute I'll explain what it adds up to.'

'Thank you, sir,' Warburton said primly.

'It adds up to this possibility,' rumbled the Inspector. 'That the sender of the message, warning Sutcliffe his ruby was in danger of being pinched, is himself a reader of the financial press. From which should arise two or three questions. Such as, for example, what people most interested in the ruby are also followers of newspapers devoted entirely to finance?'

The Sergeant nodded and Crow went on sententiously: 'Having arrived at that stage, we next proceed, by a narrowing-down process, to put our finger on the one who actually sent the letter.'

It didn't strike Sergeant Warburton that it was all going to be so easy as the Inspector made it sound. 'How do you propose to make a start in that direction, sir?' he asked.

The other indicated the anonymous message and the newspaper with a wide sweep of the arm. 'Well, I haven't been exactly idle, have I?' Adding with a jeer: 'Though no doubt you would have settled the whole blinking case by now.'

Sergeant Warburton realized he had not conveyed his enthusiastic admiration for his superior's ratiocinative talents in terms sufficiently boundless. He sighed inwardly, but it was too late now. He consoled himself with the reflection that, had he made the attempt to ingratiate himself, it would almost certainly have been received with harshly expressed contempt.

Inspector Crow was telling him: 'When you've decided to drag yourself out of your daydream, perhaps you'll condescend to listen to some instructions.'

'I am listening, sir,' Warburton said mildly.

'Thanks.' And then: 'Tonight you'll have an opportunity to doll yourself up, anyway, show yourself off in swank society, which should be a pretty sight. In other words, his nibs has invited us to this party.'

The Sergeant permitted a flicker of anticipatory pleasure to light up his face. 'That should be quite enjoyable, sir,' he said. 'White tie, I presume?'

'You can wear a length of rope round your ruddy neck for all I care,' said Crow offensively. 'Perhaps somebody might step on the end and throttle you, though I expect that's too much to hope for.'

There was a short silence, during which the Inspector lurched up from the desk and stared out of the window, sucking reflectively at his pipe. Warburton thought it was time for him to remove himself.

'Will there be anything else, sir?'

Crow regarded him hostilely and shook his head. As the other turned away, the Inspector clasped his hands behind his back and observed with deep satisfaction: 'One thing about the case, anyhow, that blasted pest Strange ain't poking his long snitch into it.'

Warburton at the door said: 'A very gratifying thought, sir.'

At that moment the telephone on the desk jangled. The Sergeant started, Crow winced, and they both regarded it with profound misgiving, The Inspector, one eye screwed up, the other glittering malevolently muttered: 'I shouldn't have said a word.'

Sergeant Warburton advanced towards the 'phone. 'Shall I take it?' he suggested helpfully. 'Er — just in case it should be — '

Crow nodded. 'If it's him, tell him I've gone to Honolulu.' And added wistfully: 'Y'never know, perhaps he might follow me there and get eaten by sharks.'

Warily, the other lifted the receiver, and while the Inspector swallowed noisily in the tense, expectant silence, said politely:

'Inspector Crow's office . . . '

* * *

Whoever may have been at the other end of Inspector Crow's telephone, however, it was not, odd perhaps as it may seem, Jimmy Strange.

Maybe it was some dear old lady inquiring about her pet poodle, or who'd lost her umbrella or merely her way; maybe it was the Commissioner himself, ringing up to ask the time. But as this adventure is unconcerned with such sundry trivia and the name of Jimmy Strange has, as was inevitable, cropped up, the whereabouts of that elusive character at this stage of the proceedings might be of some interest.

As it happens, at the precise moment when Inspector Crow, learning that the caller on the 'phone *isn't* Jimmy Strange, is releasing a mountainous sigh of thankfulness, Jimmy is leaning negligently against the bar at 'Joe's Place', smiling whimsically to himself at some passing thought which is unlikely to be in any way concerned with Inspector Crow. But his amused reflections are interrupted by a voice in his ear:

''Lo, Mr. Strange.'

Jimmy proceeds to give the owner of the voice some attention, on account of this individual being a somewhat useful contact, in fact his knowledge of what the underworld is scheming and plotting borders on the uncanny. Known as 'The Major', he is a dapper figure with iron-grey hair, twirling moustache, monocle and an unmistakable Poona accent. Apart from being a connoisseur of whisky, which vocation he follows with considerable practical purpose, he is an adept at any sort of petty swindling, from writing out rubber cheques to bilking unsuspecting hotel proprietors.

It is also said that he has on occasion put in a squeak to the police for so little a reward as a couple of drinks and a square meal. But only when he has been particularly hungry — and thirsty.

'The Major' is observing as he bathes his tonsils with the Scotch Jimmy has bought him: 'Ever been to one of Curtis Sutcliffe's parties, ol' fellah?'

Jimmy raises a quizzical eyebrow at him. 'Do I look as if I get around with the high finance crowd?'

'Frankly, ol' fellah, you look as if you'd be at home anywhere, an' with anyone. From a dive like this,' he indicates the noisy bar, 'an' its motley crew, to any stately home of England, an' the society of dukes an' duchesses — especially the latter.' Leeringly. 'What?'

'You embarrass me,' says Jimmy.

'Cosmopolitan, that's your biggest asset,' the other declares.

'Don't seem to remember being told about that.'

But 'The Major' is saying: 'Seriously, though, ol' fellah, you should go to one of Sutcliffe's little bunfights. Throws one once in a while, he does. Couple of hundred guests and everything regardless, y'know. Drink flowing like the Ganges in the rainy season. Damned good show.'

'Any pig-stickin'?' Jimmy says.

'The Major' chortles. 'Very witty. Most amusin'.'

'What else about Sutcliffe's charity bazaars?'

'Oh . . . Well, there's the Crimson Lake.' Elaborately casual. 'The ruby, don'tcherknow.'

'I know.'

The other regards him, his monocle glinting. Then leans closer and suddenly speaks from the side of his mouth. 'Matter of fact, Sutcliffe's received an anonymous warning the stone's in danger of — er — disappearing during the party he's giving tonight.'

'Just fancy,' Jimmy remarks as he takes a drink from his glass.

'Interestin', what? Scotland Yard's been given the tip.'

Jimmy waits for 'The Major' to go on. He doesn't wonder how he's picked up the information, he guesses a servant's probably chatted indiscreetly and the underworld grapevine has snapped up the scrap of gossip, borne it along the amazingly widespread ramifications of its branches until it has reached the alert ear of 'The Major'. Who continues:

'What *is* of particular interest, however, is that despite the warning the ruby has apparently not been removed to a place of greater safety, but remains where it was. Presumably in the house.'

'How come you find that so intriguing?'

The monocle glints again. 'Only it reminds me of when we used to do a spot of tiger-shootin'. We'd use bait sometimes to attract the cats to a spot covered by our guns, don'tcherknow.'

Jimmy nods.

'That's all,' the other says. 'Just thought the idea'd amuse you. I mean, you move around and it mightn't be a bad show to be on the spot tonight, just in case anything — er — happens.'

'Speaking of getting around, you aren't exactly Little Kitsy Sit-by-the-Fire yourself. Why don't you invite yourself to the party?'

'Bit embarrassin' for me an' all that if the ruby did do the Indian rope trick while I was in the vicinity. What?'

Jimmy sees his angle. He says: 'You seem pretty sure something'll crop up.'

'I didn't say that, ol' chap. Fellah can stretch his ears an' as a result reach certain conclusions. But if he's jumpin' the wrong fence, well, he's put two and two together an' sold himself the dummy. 'Fraid I'm mixin' my metaphors a trifle, but you savvy?' And he changes the subject by ostentatiously raising his empty glass. So Jimmy buys him another and 'The Major' knocks it back and fades.

Jimmy is turning over in his mind the idea, perhaps it could be amusing to pop in on Curtis Sutcliffe's party, because, though he's had no invitation, Sandra, as it happens, has. Sandra is going with some people who are upper crust socially and in the dear old City. He would like to see her face when he suddenly appeared out of the mob and asked her for the next dance. He would like to see her face anyway, it was that kind of face. And then if there's anything in this stuff 'The

Major' has been spilling about the Crimson Lake business, it would add to the interest. Especially if he should — well, happen to butt in on any little game that's going.

It occurs to Jimmy it would be useful to check up on Curtis Sutcliffe, might be an item or two about the character he isn't wise to. After all, it's only showing a polite interest in your host — even if the chap doesn't know he is your host — to learn all you can about him. So Jimmy manhandles another drink and grabs a taxi for Fleet Street.

Jimmy Strange paid off his taxi outside the *Daily Telegram* office just in time to catch Alex Connor coming out. Alex was looking larger and untidier than ever and whooped like a Sioux brave on seeing Jimmy. When it came to knowing the inside stuff about people, Connor's big ear was closer to the ground than anyone else in Fleet Street. Particularly if the ground happened to be somewhat dirty. He was on his way to a liquid lunch, but when Jimmy told him what was on his mind he took his arm and steered him to the lift and they went up to the newsroom. As newsrooms go it was quiet, and Jimmy parked himself on a desk, and when he could hear himself think, smiled at somebody's passing secretary with pretty legs, while Alex got him the file on Curtis Sutcliffe.

It was a fat file all right. Sutcliffe had stamped his dynamic personality all over the world of finance in no half-hearted way. With the press cuttings on his meteoric business career went the clippings on his social climb. His yacht, his racing stables, his country houses, villa on the Mediterranean, all the works. Plenty about the Crimson Lake ruby, too. While Jimmy was pushing his way through the stuff, Alex ambled off and returned with another file, which he slapped down on the desk alongside the other.

He watched Jimmy's face as he stared at it, a bit puzzled. The name on the file was NADIA LAROY. Which didn't mean anything to Jimmy at all. Except make him think of a name for some ice cream or something.

'Getting your names a bit mixed, Alex,

aren't you?' he said.

The other shook his head, his smile broader.

'You want the inside dirt on Sutcliffe, eh?'

Jimmy tapped the Laroy file. 'But where does she — ?'

'He was nuts about her,' Alex said.

Nadia Laroy's press clippings were mostly photographs. Photos of an extremely delectable-looking blonde. The earlier captions underneath told Jimmy she was the well-known mannequin, and he was wondering how she managed to escape his notice and wishing she hadn't. Then came some later photos of her smiling dreamily at a nice-looking dark young man with a sprinkle of confetti round his ears. The captions included his name, Alan Page. Alex Connor jabbed at him with his pipe stem.

'He used to be Sutcliffe's private secretary.'

'Like that, was it?'

'Like that,' Alex said. 'Chucked the big man she did for the other one. Married him.'

144

'What's happened to them now?'

'Girl's in New York working for some advertising firm, I believe. Boy's still around London, trying to scrape enough money to go out and join her.'

'Not much of a marriage, that.'

'Oh, I expect they write each other. Often think marriages would work out better if the husband lived in one country and the wife in another.'

'You may have something there,' Jimmy told him.

Alex grinned back at him. Then said reflectively; 'It knocked Sutcliffe all of a doodah. Some say he's never forgiven either of 'em. Hardly credit it, eh? Fact. All that dough, power couldn't buy him that little doll.' He jabbed Nadia Laroy's photo with his pipe.

''Course, Sutcliffe kicked out young Page on the spot. Helluva shindy. Real vicious he was. S'pose it hit his pride and all that.'

'Cosy little drama,' Jimmy said, tapping a cigarette on his case and lighting it.

The other puffed away thoughtfully for a moment at his pipe.

Idly he turned some of the cuttings from the big file and picked out a photo of Sutcliffe.

'Talking of dramatics,' he said slowly. 'I always have the feeling one of these days I'll see that dial over a caption of quite a different kind.'

Jimmy eyed him narrowly. 'How different?'

'Dunno,' he muttered. 'Something — *unpleasant*.'

★　★　★

Curtis Sutcliffe's house in Highgate was a whacking great white mansion of a place standing in its own grounds, screened from the road by trees, a wide drive curving up to its massive porch. When Jimmy arrived he found the drive already packed with opulent-looking cars, and he caught the sound of a dance orchestra giving out as he nosed his own car into a vacant space and cut the engine. He'd carefully left his coat and hat behind, and found no difficulty at all in conveying to a watchful manservant the impression that he was merely returning from a gulp of fresh air or a look at the stars or something.

He was lighting a cigarette — standing a little apart from the crush of people milling around the brilliantly lit spacious hall — and wondering which way the bar was, when he caught sight of a face that caused his eyes to narrow into speculative slits. It was him all right. No doubt about that. Jimmy exhaled slowly and was considering the possibilities the other's presence might indicate, when a character with receding hair approached and eyed him expectantly over thick-lensed glasses.

'Inspector Crow?' he asked quietly.

Jimmy had been given a number of doubtful names in his time, with invariably disastrous results to the giver, but had never anticipated being mistaken for the dear Inspector. However, nothing ever caught him off his balance and he said promptly:

'I'm his deputy. Inspector Crow's detained and may be rather late. The name is Strange.'

'I'm Rayner. Mr. Sutcliffe's secretary.'

Jimmy said: 'Good.' He decided Curtis Suteliffe had definitely taken no chances over the man he'd hired in place of Alan Page.

Rayner was a weak-looking individual with about as much appeal as a jellyfish. He calculated there was practically no risk whatever of his running off with anybody's girlfriend. Except, maybe, another jellyfish. And she'd have to be frantically hard up.

Rayner looked as if he was washing his hands without using soap and said:

'Mr. Sutcliffe is in the library. He would like to see you, I'm sure.'

Jimmy asked: 'Would he have any drink there?'

The secretary looked slightly startled, but recovered himself to smile thinly. 'I think you'll find Mr. Sutcliffe will be able to offer you some refreshment.'

As Jimmy followed him he pondered, with a certain amusement, on the whereabouts of the expected Inspector Crow. It wasn't like him to be unpunctual and it seemed plain he should have put in an appearance by now. He wondered idly what his reaction would be when he did arrive and discovered who was keeping his place warm for him. Jimmy thought he could guess all right and chuckled inwardly with anticipation. Meantime, he'd look as much like a cop as he could and keep his eyes and ears open. He fancied somehow 'The Major' had, without knowing it, given him quite a tip.

Curtis Sutcliffe greeted him with a show of affability and, with a cigar that looked about three feet long stuck in his face, began pouring out drinks. As he handed Jimmy his, he said:

'I thought we might have a chat, and if there's anything you'd like to know that would be useful . . . '

He left the rest of the sentence suspended on the cigar smoke and looked helpful.

Jimmy let his gaze take in the surroundings over the rim of his glass. And Curtis Sutcliffe's library was something you really couldn't miss. Luxury literally leered at you from every side. Rich oak panelling from floor to ceiling, curtains and tapestries that fairly glowed with colour, and a carpet so thick you felt you were walking in velvet up to your ankles.

After a moment, Jimmy though he should say something suitable to the role he'd taken on, so he said: 'Where's the ruby tucked away?'

The other crossed obediently to the wide fireplace and pressed somewhere underneath the massive, ornately carved mantelpiece. At his touch a section of the woodwork, about nine inches square sprang open to reveal a small wall safe. 'Neat, isn't it?' Sutcliffe said over his shoulder. He went on: 'Needless to say, we in this room are the only people who know of its existence.'

Jimmy glanced casually at Rayner, who'd remained unobtrusively in the background, making no contribution to the conversation and doing precious little to improve the scenery either. Now, however, he ventured to put in a word:

'*And* my predecessor.'

'Ah, yes,' Sutcliffe murmured, as if reminded of the fact. His face took on an abstract expression, then he seemed to dismiss whatever it was he'd been thinking and bent slightly in an attitude of concentration before the safe. Came a sharp metallic click and the safe door swung back. Sutcliffe rummaged inside and after a moment held the Crimson Lake under the light for Jimmy's inspection. It was some ruby and no mistake, glowing up at him like something alive. And Sutcliffe chose the moment to say, conversationally:

'By the way, Mr. Rayner's — ah — predecessor already referred to happens to be one of my guests tonight.' He was smiling slowly as he spoke, though it seemed to Jimmy his smile didn't quite match up with his lidless eyes. 'Yes,' he went on smoothly, 'the circumstances of his leaving were somewhat painful to me at the time, but I hope all that's forgotten now. And forgiven. His presence here is in fact an attempt on my part to persuade him to let bygones be bygones. Page his name is, Alan Page. Charming and very capable young man.'

Jimmy didn't say anything. He didn't think it necessary to mention it was young Page he'd recognized immediately on his arrival. And he didn't think it necessary, either, to mention Sutcliffe's story hardly added up to the stuff Alex Connor had handed him, or that he was beginning to see the wheels going round. He preferred to sit tight and wait to put his spoke in and upset the applecart when the moment was exactly the right moment.

Curtis Sutcliffe was still talking:

'I feel I was perhaps too harsh on him. After all, one shouldn't forget the time when oneself was young — ' He broke off and turned to Rayner: 'Mr. Page arrived yet?'

'Er — yes,' the other nodded.

'Perhaps you'd find him presently? Say I'll be glad for him to join me over a drink.'

'Very well.' He hesitated for a moment, then muttered: 'If you'll excuse me, there are one or two matters I have to attend to.'

After he'd gone, Jimmy said:

'Presumably your secretary knows why the — er — police are here?'

'Yes. No one else has been told anything about it, of course.'

Sutcliffe gave Jimmy a glance from behind his cigar and then crossed to the safe with the ruby. As he bent again to close it up, he threw over his shoulder: 'As an added precaution I switch the combination every two or three days. Only Rayner and I know what it is.'

'Good idea, so long as neither of you jot it down to leave about for anyone else to see.'

The other replied the combination was simple enough to remember, no need to make a note of it, you just kept it in your head.

Jimmy was beginning to think there wasn't anything else he could do there in the library, and was deciding to beat it and take a look round for Sandra when the 'phone rang.

Curtis Sutcliffe answered it. 'Speaking . . .' Then shot a look at Jimmy. 'This may interest you,' he said. 'It sounds like Inspector Crow. Seems his car's broken down or something.' He turned to the receiver again as Jimmy quickly crossed over. He wanted to grab that 'phone before Sutcliffe said too much. Already he was saying: 'Your deputy's here, Inspector, anyway, so everything's under control.'

'All right,' Jimmy said briskly, politely wrenching the phone out of the other's grasp. 'I'll talk to him.'

Sutcliffe showed his dislike at being shoved around in his own library, but Jimmy wasn't noticing. He was grinning into the mouthpiece.

'Yes, Crow, old bird, it's Strange — just keeping an eye on things for you.'

The Inspector must have thought the line was playing him tricks. 'Who's that speaking?' he demanded, disbelief in his tone.

'You heard.'

'What the — ? How the — ?' Crow spluttered.

'Take your time,' Jimmy cooed.

'I'll — I'll — What the hell are you doing posing as a detective?'

'You've been doing it for years. Why shouldn't I try?' He chuckled at the throttling noises that came over the wire.

'Tell me,' he went on pleasantly, 'when may we expect you? Not that you need bother really. I mean now you know I'm here, why not go home, have an early night?'

'I'll be up there to deal with you just as soon as I can get hold of another flaming car,' grated the Inspector.

'Expect I'll be waiting, you impetuous creature. But try not to hurry too much, you don't want to ditch another car. Might break your neck — I hope.' And rang off, smiling blandly at a slightly mystified-looking Curtis Sutcliffe.

A few moments later Jimmy left the other in the library and pushed off in the general direction of Sandra and the bar, whichever he happened to meet up with first. On his way he saw Rayner talking to Alan Page, and they passed him, presumably going to the library. The secretary peered at him shortsightedly and gave him a nod of acknowledgement. Jimmy stared after them thoughtfully and decided he'd have to give up the idea of looking for Sandra for the moment. He'd have time only for a drink and that was all. He was back within a few minutes by the wide staircase and, lighting a cigarette, stood eyeing the celebrities, and those who thought they were, in case he might see Sandra and, at the same time, keeping his attention on the passage leading to the library.

Presently two things happened almost simultaneously.

He caught sight of Sandra and — as she stared at him unbelievingly and then came over, smiling with excited surprise — Alan Page appeared.

'Jimmy,' Sandra began. 'Where on earth did you — ?'

'Listen, darling,' he cut in quickly. 'Just pretend you don't want to ask me one teensy question, but would love to be introduced to this nice young man.'

While she was still wide-eyed at him, he took her arm and led her purposefully across to Alan Page.

'Your name's Page?'

The other said, 'Yes,' slowly, saw Sandra and definitely brightened. Jimmy went on, a sharp urgency in his voice: 'You don't know it — yet — but you're in a jam, and I'm on your side. Come over here, I want to talk to you.'

While Page was recovering from his surprise and Sandra continued to gaze at him in utter bewilderment, he led the way to a secluded corner behind the staircase.

'Look here,' Page found his voice. 'Who are you? I don't quite — '

'Shut up and listen,' Jimmy said briskly, 'if you want to know something for your own damned good. First,' he went on, while the other faced him blankly, 'hasn't it struck you as slightly incongruous your being here tonight?'

Page frowned, then muttered slowly:

'I don't understand what you're driving at, unless you — you mean about my having been Curtis Sutcliffe's secretary, and — '

'And got kicked out on account of Mrs. Page — Nadia Laroy that was,' Jimmy snapped impatiently. 'I know. So I'm asking you again; doesn't his invitation strike you as being right out of character?'

'Well . . . ' Page said uneasily, 'since you know so much — he 'phoned and said would I forget what had happened, let bygones be bygones? He said that was

157

the way he felt about it, he wanted to bury the hatchet, so would I come to this party and we'd shake hands over a drink? So' — he shrugged — 'I don't go around bearing malice, wearing a chip on my shoulder, and — here I am.'

Jimmy said: 'You didn't think his idea might be to bury the hatchet in *you*?'

The other looked at him sharply, then at Sandra, who gave the appearance of someone who'd stumbled into the middle of a film without the faintest idea of what the plot was all about. Page said to Jimmy: 'What d'you mean?'

'Never mind.' Jimmy waved the idea aside. 'So you've been having a drink with him and he's been all magnanimous all over the library. Quite like old times I shouldn't wonder.'

Page grinned slightly. 'Roughly that,' he said. 'He asked after Nadia — my wife, you know.'

'I know,' Jimmy reminded him.

'He knows,' Sandra said, but Jimmy's smile was bleak.

'Matter of fact, it was quite like old times,' Page was saying and laughed as if something had amused him. 'He even asked me to show him an old handkerchief trick that used to peeve him because he never could do it.'

'What handkerchief trick?'

'You tie it so it looks like a rabbit. He always made a hash of it. He did when he tried it just now.'

Sandra noticed the handkerchief protruding from his breast pocket looked a trifle crumpled.

Jimmy's face wore a frozen look. Then: 'I'm interested in tricks,' he said softly. 'Show.'

The other smiled and proceeded to oblige. As he pulled the handkerchief out, something flipped from its folds and lay in the palm of his hand. He stared at it stupidly.

'Some trick,' murmured Jimmy, as the Crimson Lake ruby glimmered up at them. He grabbed it and said to Sandra: 'Get him out of here and wait for me in my car.' He handed her his keys.

As she hesitated, trying to make sense of it all, he urged: 'Move, darling, get him out,' and with a glance at young Page, who was still glassy-eyed as if he'd just been kicked smartly in the stomach by a recalcitrant mule, was gone. Jimmy flattered himself his was an open mind at all times and so what he encountered when he reached the library made him halt in his stride for only a fraction of a second. Then he crossed to Curtis Sutcliffe, who was slumped over his writing desk very dead indeed.

A bullet had smacked into him behind his left ear and the marks of burning round the wound showed whoever fired the shot hadn't taken any chance about missing him. Jimmy jabbed a bell push and noted the scattered papers and capsized inkstand, from which green ink had spilled and was staining the rich carpet. He swung his gaze to the wall safe, which gaped wide open, and then Rayner hurried into the room. The secretary stared unbelievingly at the figure sprawled at the desk and looked as if he was about to collapse. Jimmy rasped at him:

'Snap out of it, Rayner.'

The other appeared to pull himself

together. 'What — what happened?' he muttered dazedly.

'Plenty,' Jimmy snapped. 'You'd better call a doctor.' He watched Rayner move like a sleepwalker to the 'phone and lift the receiver. 'Not that he'll mean a thing,' he added smoothly. '*You made too good a job of it!*'

There was a moment's deathly silence as Rayner blinked over the receiver. Then: 'What — what d'you mean?'

Jimmy said evenly:

'Only you knew that combination beside Sutcliffe. Trouble was when you opened the safe you were too late. He'd already planted it on young Page, which was something you hadn't bargained for.'

He thrust his hand into his pocket and flipped the Crimson Lake on to the desk. 'That's what you were after, wasn't it?' And he took out his case and lit a cigarette.

The other's face was drained putty-colour. 'I — I haven't been in here since Page left.'

'No?' Jimmy smiled at him thinly. 'Take a look at your shirt-cuff.'

Rayner sucked in his breath and peered shortsightedly at his hand still clutching the 'phone. *The cuff showing above it was stained with bright green ink.* There came a quick movement as Rayner dropped the 'phone and a gun appeared in his hand. It was a sinister-looking job, with a silencer fitted to the barrel. 'Move an inch,' he mouthed, 'and I'll blow you to hell too.'

'Take it easy,' Jimmy drawled through a puff of cigarette smoke, as his gaze flickered over the other's shoulder in the direction of the door. 'Someone's watching.'

Involuntarily Rayner turned his head, to recoil with a hunted look as Inspector Crow filled the doorway, Sergeant Warburton behind him. He swung his gun towards them — which was a silly thing for him to do under the circumstances, for Jimmy, moving with the speed of light, draped a punch that would have felled an ox neatly against the side of his jaw.

★   ★   ★

'Rayner planned the whole setup with the idea suspicion would fall on you,' Jimmy said to Page some time later, as he turned the car on to the St. John's Wood Road. Page was squeezing Sandra, who sat between them, against Jimmy, who didn't mind it at all. He went on: 'The fact that you wouldn't have the ruby on you, Rayner thought, wouldn't necessarily clear you, the cops could argue you'd merely hidden it to collect later. But what he didn't know was that Sutcliffe had invited you for the sole purpose of planting the ruby on you, then accusing you of having pinched it.'

'Charming thought,' Sandra said.

'Motive, of course: revenge?' Page said.

'Just that. He'd concocted some anonymous warning as an excuse to have the police on the spot when his scheme went into operation. Crow muttered something to me about he suspected it was phoney, matter of fact. But anyway, Sutcliffe planted the stone when you were doing that handkerchief trick.'

'I think I know how he must have done it,' the other said. 'When he gave me back the handkerchief.'

'Maybe,' Jimmy said. 'Then Rayner, the

moment you'd gone, pops into the library, deals with Sutcliffe — and then discovers he's done the dirty deed for nothing. No ruby. So he beats it. The rest . . . ' He allowed the rest to melt into a puff of cigarette smoke. Then he grinned at Sandra. 'All of which, I hope, will be a warning not to go to rich financier's parties. But to stay home with Daddy.'

'All of which would be heaven,' Sandra threw back at him, 'if Daddy stayed home too.'

5

The Man at the Piano

The boat-train wasn't crowded and the two men had the first-class compartment to themselves. They sat facing each other in their corners hunched behind evening papers. There was a certain tenseness about their attitude, an alertness that made their preoccupation with their papers appear superficial. From each thin mouth a cigarette drooped. Each face was shadowed by a soft hat pulled down over the eyes, each chin sunk in the turned-up collar of their overcoats. Neither appeared to carry any luggage, the racks overhead were empty.

Presently the smaller of the two men stirred. Stubbing out his cigarette he got up.

'Think I'll take a look along the train now.'

Without raising his eyes from his paper, the other nodded and the small man went out, pulling the door shut after him.

He was back in a few minutes. He was smiling, not a particularly pleasant smile. He said:

'I've spotted him. Just along the corridor. And he's alone.'

'Bit of luck,' the other muttered.

'Yeh. I reckon we'd better fix him now.'

'Don't be a fool!'

'Why not, while the going's good — '

'Shut up and sit down.'

The small man obeyed and lit a cigarette. His hand was shaking slightly. The other leaned across and said:

'If we fix him now, someone may find him before the train gets in. We don't want that. So we wait till we're just running into London. Less chance of him being found until the train's in the station and we've scrammed. Besides there's a tunnel just outside the terminus. See?'

The small man nodded.

'I get it. Drown any noise.'

His companion gave him a cold stare.

'I thought you might catch on,' he said

with mirthless sarcasm and returned to his paper. The train roared on towards London and the small man hunched in his corner staring out at the gathering dusk.

Some time later the other man glanced at his wristwatch.

'Should be in soon. Boat-trains are always on the dot. Better get into the corridor, ready for the tunnel.'

They went out of the compartment. The train whistled shrilly. The small man said: 'This'll be it, eh?'

The other man nodded. 'Come on,' he said shortly, and moved down the corridor. They passed two or three compartments that were half empty and gained one whose solitary occupant, in the farther corner, was absorbed in a novel. He was a biggish man, dark and flashily good-looking. He wore a big astrakhan-collared overcoat, which was open and a silk scarf tied loosely round his neck. The luggage rack above him was crammed with opulent-looking suitcases, and on the seat beside him were scattered magazines and newspapers.

He glanced up with casual curiosity as the two men entered, closing the door behind them. The train gave a shriek and thundered through the tunnel.

★ ★ ★

The elements of the underworld are caught up and carried along by numerous crosscurrents. Some move of their own initiative and impulse. Others just drift. But always the direction is the same, all currents merge into the deep and dark waters of crime. A popular port of call for many members of this brotherhood of oddly assorted driftwood and riffraff is the Greek Street caravanserai known as 'Joe's Place'. Here, as has been noted before, you may, while downing your favourite potion, rub shoulders on the one side with a small-time music-hall performer or a prosperous-looking 'con' man, and, on the other, with a smart little newspaper reporter or a hatchet-faced mobster.

Tonight, however, it is early. 'Joe's Place' is slack. A couple of men are assisting each other prop up the bar, while the barman is listening morosely to the racing results which are coming over a tinny radio behind him.

' . . . And that is the end of the sports news,' the immaculate, carefully modulated voice announces.

'Thank yer very much!' observes the bartender with great bitterness. 'I 'opes they arrested that ruddy 'orse for loitering!'

One of the men on the clients' side of the bar, wearing black tie and impeccably white shirt, soft black hat tilted rakishly over one eye chuckles and is about to commiserate with the other's bad luck when the impersonal tones over the radio continue:

'Here is a police message. Mr. Harry Bell, an American passenger on the evening boat-train from Southampton, was attacked and knocked unconscious by unknown assailants as the train was approaching London. It is believed two men were concerned in the attack. Apparently robbery was not the motive and Mr. Bell was possibly mistaken for someone else. Anybody travelling by this train who may have witnessed the attack, or may give any information regarding it, is asked to communicate with Scotland Yard. Telephone Whitehall 1212.'

'Harry Bell?' queries the other customer, a thin character, 'American music-hall act, isn't he?'

The man in evening dress nods, drawing thoughtfully at his cigarette. The radio voice proceeds smoothly:

'And now, as we have a minute or two before the next part of the programme, here is a gramophone record . . . ' rattling off the names of some unpronounceable foreign performer and equally unpronounceable piece of music. Follows the sound of some incredibly dismal piano-pounding and the barman screws up his face in anguish and snaps the radio off.

'Aw, for crying out loud! I'd rather 'ear the racing results all over again, even though I 'ave gone down the drain!'

'Got no soul, that's your trouble,' smiles the thin individual, whose name is Frankie Willis and who happens to be a cardsharper by profession. He turns to his neighbour. 'Funny . . . that chap being knocked about like that.'

'Don't expect 'e saw the joke!' cuts in the barman.

'What's so amusing about it?' says the individual in the black hat, through a cloud of cigarette smoke.

'Well . . . you see, I happened to be on that train this evening. You know — er — business.'

The man beside him smiles understandingly.

The bartender chortles: 'Was it you wot clonked him 'cos he *did* find the lady?'

Frankie Willis laughs genially. 'Matter of fact, yours truly didn't — er — operate at all. Saw a couple of Zucci's boys on the train, so decided to lie low.'

'Zucci's boys?' says the man in evening dress, raising a quizzical eyebrow.

The other nods. 'I always feel kind of nervous when that bunch are around.'

'Don't blame you neither,' mutters the barman.

'Though I don't think they . . . No, it wouldn't have been them.'

'What's on your mind?' asks that soft

yet curiously knife-edged voice through another puff of cigarette-smoke. 'You think they'd nothing to do with the Bell business?'

'Robbery with violence isn't their usual racket.'

'Dope's Zucci's line,' declares the man behind the bar emphatically. 'Allus 'as bin.'

Willis nods. 'That's right.'

'But this *wasn't* robbery,' comes the quiet, almost gentle reminder in his ear. 'You heard what the radio said.'

'You've said it.'

'Besides . . .'

'Besides what?'

The eyes shadowed by the black hat are suddenly enigmatic. 'Just an idea I had.'

Willis says: 'Well, anyway, I never saw anyone else on the train who might've done the job, and I know most of the boys.'

The bartender, holding up a glass he is polishing to the light and squinting through it, observes: 'Maybe there's more in it than wot meets the eye. One thing,' he goes on, 'that Zucci's a rat.'

'You got something there,' says Frankie Willis.

'I don't mind most things — arter all, a feller's got ter live, though don't ask me why — but dope's *dirty*.'

The other says:

'Bell's appearing at the 'Coronet', isn't he?'

'Dunno,' the barman replies, then chortles: 'P'raps he's beat up too bad to appear anywhere, except the 'orspital!'

The one in evening dress glances at his wristwatch, as if suddenly reminded of something.

'Which reminds me,' he says, 'time I beat it.' And drains his drink.

The barman gives him a surprised look. 'You *are* 'opping it in an' 'urry. Where's the ruddy fire?'

'In my girlfriend's eyes! Good night.'

The bartender guffaws and calls after him:

''Night, Mister Strange.'

'And if it's the girl I saw you with last time,' Frankie Willis calls out, 'give her a kiss for me!'

Jimmy Strange turned out of 'Joe's

173

Place' and moved swiftly down Greek Street towards Shaftesbury Avenue. He grinned to himself as it occurred to him that the girl he was heading towards was, as it happened, the same Frankie Willis had met with him on another occasion. Sandra — and he was on his way to join her for dinner at the new little restaurant she'd recently discovered on the other side of Shaftesbury Avenue. Then they were going on to the 'Coronet's' second house.

It was the mention of the music-hall that had jerked Jimmy out of the reverie in which he'd been indulging regarding a certain character named Zucci and Harry Bell. It was the American Sandra had specially wanted to see. He was supposed to be the latest thing in crooners-at-the-piano type, and Sandra could do with a sentimental song or two as well as any girl. Any girl that is, who's either in or just out of love. Sandra, of course, was in love, though she was doing her best at the moment with little apparent effect to break herself of the habit, because she had a pretty good notion being in love with a character like Jimmy Strange

174

wasn't calculated to get her very far. In the direction of the preacher, anyway.

As for Jimmy, he had shown a mild interest at the prospect of viewing Mr. Bell at the piano, even if he anticipated witnessing the performance from a somewhat more prosaic slant. The gentleman's face — which he'd noted in the Press, advertising his forthcoming London appearance — had at once struck a reminiscent chord. He'd seen it before some time back in New York. But, so far as his memory went, the face hadn't been bent over a keyboard then.

And now the news of the business on the boat-train, plus the information from Frankie Willis that Zucci's boys had been around at the time, added up to something. Jimmy thought he would like to know what.

He went into the restaurant and found Sandra already at the table in the corner, with a waiter hovering by. She was looking too lovely to be true, which was a way Sandra had of looking at all times. She stared at him, slightly incredulously, as he sat down.

He said:

'Hello, darling. Glad to see me?'

She said:

'What on earth's happened?'

'Umph?'

'You've only kept me waiting five minutes. Usually it's more like five hours — if you remember to turn up at all! What went wrong, your favourite bar run out of drink, or something?'

'You're being very amusing, darling,' he smiled at her. 'Though inclined to exaggerate slightly. Maybe I am a little late sometimes, but you know how it is, a chap gets tied up with — er — circumstances, and has to stick around till he's undone all the knots.'

'So long as you don't get roped up so tightly sometime you *can't* wriggle your way out, I suppose it's all right,' she said.

'Yours are the only bonds I find difficult to slip.'

'Maybe you haven't tried very hard.'

'I've tried like hell,' he grinned at her. 'But somehow I just can't get away.' He leaned forward and added confidentially: 'You know what?'

176

'Tell me.'

'I don't think I want to get away.'

Her eyes were very tender. She said softly:

'You're a damned liar, Jimmy Strange. And I'm a damned fool to believe a word of it, but would you mind saying all that over again?'

He chuckled. 'In the taxi, on the way to the 'Coronet', I'll confide in you even more closely, if you like. That's why I got here on the dot tonight,' he went on, blandly disregarding the fact that he had, in fact, arrived five minutes late. 'I didn't want you to miss the show.'

She surveyed him with amusement.

'What's on your mind, Jimmy?' she said.

'You,' he said lightly. 'Always.'

'What's so interesting about the show at the 'Coronet',' she pursued, 'that *you* don't want to be late for it?'

He contrived to stare at her with an expression that combined the utmost innocence with that of dumbfounded bewilderment — for him something of an achievement.

'They're not such exciting turns as all that,' she went on, her eyes slightly puzzled and speculative. 'A comedian, a trapeze act — there's a little blonde in that who's very cute, I believe — '

'She'd never fall for me.'

'And, of course, this newest heart-throb and lonesome girls' delight, Harry Bell. But I can't imagine you'd be crazy over him.'

Jimmy said:

'No, I wouldn't be crazy over him.' And left it at that.

The 'Coronet' was jammed, and when Harry Bell's programme number was illuminated in the proscenium frames there was prolonged thunder of anticipatory applause. The enthusiastic storm died as, from behind the curtain, still down, came the tinkling of a piano. The curtain rose and the spotlight lit a dark man in dinner jacket at a white baby grand. The cut of his clothes was inclined to be flashy, and an artificial carnation made a crimson splotch on his lapel. He smiled at the audience and went into his routine.

His personality was pretty powerful and virile, it overflowed across the footlights in waves. As he bent over the piano it seemed to be a mere toy in his hands moving only a little over the keys. His voice was huskily resonant and his Broadway accent not unpleasing. He sang in an intimate tone, as if he was passing on the innermost secrets of his aching heart. All his songs spoke of disappointed love and pent-up longing for the right girl to come along. It was all very slick and effective. He showed no signs of the attack that had been made on him on the boat-train.

Glancing round him, Jimmy observed everyone was listening with rapt attention. Sandra seemed suitably impressed, though she caught his glance and smiled at him as if to say she was only temporarily and superficially charmed. He grinned back at her and lit a cigarette.

Harry Bell sang a handful of songs and was forced to throw in a couple of encores before they'd let him go. He took a bow before the curtain and the applause lasted until the curtain went up again on a couple of knockabout comedians.

Jimmy stirred in his seat.

Sandra said:

'Thirsty?'

He nodded. He said:

'You wouldn't do so bad yourself as a mind-reading act.' He patted her hand. 'I'll be right back.'

She looked at him disbelievingly. She said:

'Just in case you *should* happen to remember me somewhere around midnight, I'll have gone home to bed. Don't bother to 'phone and wake me to ask if I got back all right, you never sound sincere.'

'I'm beginning to wonder what you find attractive about me.'

'I refrain from making the obvious answer, but you have my permission to guess what I'm thinking.'

Deliberately misunderstanding her, he said:

'Darling, you mustn't flatter me so much.' And was gone.

In the bar, behind the stalls, he knocked back two double Scotches with alacrity and precision, set the pert, over-lipsticked barmaid's heart bumping with a devastating smile (he was thinking about something quite different at the time) and went swiftly, purposefully, out, down by the side of the theatre and found the stage door.

To the grizzled, bespectacled stage door keeper he said briskly:

'Mr. Bell's expecting me, I'm from the *Gazette*.'

'I think he's just off the stage, sir. If you'll hold on I'll give his dressing room a ring.'

He turned to the switchboard, adjusted his spectacles, and in a moment was speaking into the telephone:

'Mr. Bell, sir? Gentleman here from the *Gazette* to see you . . . Yes, sir . . . Certainly, sir.' He hung up and said: 'Mr. Bell'll see you.'

Jimmy smiled. He'd little doubt that the American would turn away a prospective interview with the Press The doorkeeper jerked a thumb over his shoulder. 'Through this door just facing you, sir, turn right, along the passage and first door you come to — Number One dressing room.'

He gave the man a tip — 'Thank you, sir' — and went through the door. Grinning amiably, he pushed past a group of chorus girls who, got up vaguely to resemble somewhat scantily-clad butter-flies, were hovering round a notice board and grumbling shrilly about an early rehearsal-call next morning, and made his way to Number One dressing room.

Harry Bell greeted him with easy affability. He had changed into a silk dressing gown of vivid design and a long cigar shifted from one side of his mouth to the other as he talked.

'Always glad to say 'hello' to you newspaper boys. Can you use a drink?'

'I can.'

Diamonds flashed in a couple of large rings on his fingers and a massive gold watch clamped to his wrist by a heavy gold bracelet glittered as he mixed a whisky-and-soda and handed it over. He mixed one for himself.

'Good luck.'

Jimmy murmured a suitable response. Followed an appropriate pause, then the other put down his glass with an appreciative sigh. 'That's better.' Pulling expansively at his cigar, he drawled: 'Now what d'you want to know about little me?'

'Well,' Jimmy said casually, 'naturally my paper's interested in this business that happened to you on the train.'

The man's eyes narrowed and he regarded the end of his cigar for a moment. He shrugged and said smiling: 'It was nothing.'

'Couldn't have been exactly fun for you, all the same.'

'It could have been worse.'

'They didn't beat you up so badly to stop you doing your show, anyway.'

'No, a knock on the bean which put me out, that was all.'

Jimmy said over the rim of his glass: 'Wonder who they mistook you for?'

'Uhuh?'

'They didn't rob you or anything — '

'No, no,' Bell muttered evasively. 'Definitely a case of mistaken identity.'

'Too bad you look like somebody else.'

The other nodded, smiling thinly.

Jimmy went on half musingly: 'Wonder

who Zucci's boys had in mind?'

The American's reaction was instantaneous. 'How the hell d'you know who — ?' he rasped, then checked himself and asked carelessly:

'Er — who did you say?'

'Zucci.'

Bell produced a silk monogrammed handkerchief and wiped his fingers where his drink had slopped over them. 'And who is — er — Zucci?'

'Runs a dope racket in this town.' Jimmy lit a cigarette. 'But you wouldn't know about that.'

'I guess not. But say . . . I'm kind of interested in this. Tell me, what makes you think it was this guy — what was his name again?'

'I'll spell it for you.' Jimmy did with elaborate care, adding to himself; As if you didn't know!

'Why d'you think he had anything to do with me being slugged?'

'I'm told a couple of his boys travelled on the same train.'

'Just that?'

'Just that.'

'You seem to know quite a bit about things, don't you?' The cigar was still, the light blue eyes above it were narrowed.

Jimmy said easily: 'We newspaper chaps get around.'

'I'll say.'

There was a little silence while Harry Bell gulped the rest of his drink. He said:

'Well, now, look . . . I wonder if you'd excuse me? Maybe you could call in some other time and I can spill you all you want about myself?'

'Whatever you say.'

The other passed his hand over his brow and closed his eyes as if in pain. Jimmy's private opinion was that he was overacting it a bit.

'Got a bit of headache coming on I guess. After-effects, y'know. I'd like to get back to my hotel and rest.'

Jimmy nodded. From the door he said:

'See you some other time.'

'That'll be swell. So long.'

As Jimmy passed the stage-door keeper's cubbyhole on his way out, the old chap was at his switchboard and speaking into the telephone:

'Soho 2323 . . . ? Will you hold on.'

Jimmy paused and ostentatiously tapped the ash off his cigarette into an old, battered ashtray on the cubbyhole window ledge. The doorkeeper flicked a switch and spoke again into the receiver:

'Your Soho number, Mr. Bell.'

As, peering inquiringly over his spectacles, he turned towards him, Jimmy muttered a loud exclamation of annoyance.

'Damn! I've left my gloves behind.' He grimaced in exasperation for the other's benefit and said: 'I'll just pop back and get 'em.'

'Orlright, sir,' the man nodded. 'Mr. Bell's on the 'phone at the moment.'

'Shan't bother him at all,' Jimmy reassured him quickly and retraced his steps, muttering loudly: 'Can't think what could have made me so careless!'

He was back within a few minutes.

'Find your gloves orlright, sir?'

Without batting an eyelid, Jimmy said brightly:

'Believe it or not, but I never brought any with me. Just remembered it. Silly of me, eh? Good night.' And with a genial grin he was gone. But there was no smile in his eyes as he turned out of the stage door and went swiftly up the street. On the corner stood a telephone box.

★ ★ ★

Inspector Crow was working late again.

The room was thick with acrid smoke from the blackened, stubby briar clamped between his teeth as he bent over his desk, beetling ginger brows drawn together in concentration. The telephone at his elbow jangled and, with a muttered imprecation, he levered himself up from the heavy dossier spread before him and grabbed the receiver.

As the voice over the wire vibrated against his eardrum, his great jaws tightened so that his pipe stem was in danger of being snapped in two.

'Only a blasted pest like you would think of ringing me at this time of night,' he barked.

'Ah,' the voice mocked him, 'that's what comes of being the brightest gem at the 'Yard'. Crow, old bird, the Commissioner's white-headed boy and teacher's little pet — you're indispensable.'

'Cut the eyewash and get to the point.'

'Listen to the great detective!' Jimmy enthused in affected admiration. 'Wasting no words, swiftly, ruthlessly, unerringly he cuts to the root of the trouble to the amazement and applause of all beholders.'

The veins were standing out on the Inspector's temples. His eyes were popping, his collar appeared to be strangling him.

'Ah, to possess a master-mind such as yours,' the cooing tones continued. 'To know that when crime stalks abroad and the dark horror of lawlessness looms over the city, it's you they send for to clean up the mess. The omnipotent Inspector Crow ... And what happens? Why, things are a hell of a lot worse than they were before!'

'You — you — !' spluttered Crow, inarticulate with rage.

'However,' went on Jimmy calmly, 'there is a certain endearing charm about

188

you, despite your hideous exterior, which occasionally prompts me to direct your flat-footed steps along the path of promotion. In other words, you nightmarish old gargoyle, I've got a pinch for you. All tied up. All you've got to do is lurch in and claim the credit.'

The other was still making horrible noises at the back of his throat.

'I thought you'd be pleased,' Jimmy said urbanely. He added: 'Know a gentleman by the name of Zucci?'

The gargling noise stopped abruptly.

'Thought the name would strike a chord. He's the egg you're going to crack.'

'Zucci,' the Inspector muttered, his breathing a little less laboured. 'You think you can — ?'

'Tonight, at, let's say midnight, that's a nice dramatic hour, you toddle into his office at that night-club of his — '

'The 'Black Lizard' '

'And catch him with the goods. How's that suit you?'

'You sound damned sure of yourself,' grunted Crow suspiciously.

'*You'd* be sure if you knew what I know.'

'What *do* you know, and *how* do you — ?' the other demanded, his voice rising angrily.

Jimmy chuckled softly. He said:

'Now don't start chewing your telephone, you may need it again.'

'I insist on you telling me where you get your information from, you ruddy smartie!' bellowed Crow.

'Since you ask me so nicely, I'll tell you. I listen to the radio, and use my bean.'

'One of these days. Mr. Clever — '

'By the way,' Jimmy interrupted him calmly, 'you reach Zucci's office from an alley at the back of the club. Up a fire escape, Another thing . . . try and memorize this little ditty.' He whistled a snatch of one of the popular songs Harry Bell had sung. 'Get it? Or has it gone right through and out the other ear? Not much in the way to stop it, I know. Listen some more.'

He began to whistle the tune again, but the roaring at the other end drowned his efforts. He said:

'Of course, if you can't appreciate my performance, no use continuing. However, I hope some of it's sunk in, because that's the tip-off.'

'Tip-off?'

'When you hear that tune coming from Zucci's office, you pop in.'

'Does that mean,' queried Crow heavily, 'you'll be there to give us the signal — *in person?*'

'You sound as if you hope I will.'

'Nothing would give me greater pleasure. And if — in the struggle when we pinch Zucci, you should happen — accidentally — to get knocked on the head, I'll be a helluva lot more pleased!'

'You're *too* kind. Maybe I'll be around. But get this, you bone-headed baboon, if you're out to grab Zucci — don't butt in before the whistle.'

The Inspector raved with affronted incoherence for fully half a minute before realizing Jimmy Strange had hung up on him. With a crash that nearly shattered the instrument he slammed down his receiver and rang savagely for Sergeant Warburton.

'You wish to see me, sir?'

'No, I *don't*!' barked Crow. 'But unfortunately for me, you happen to be my assistant, so at times I've got to see you.' He added with extreme bitterness: 'I keep my calls on you down to a minimum!'

'Thank you, sir,' said Sergeant Warburton.

The Inspector glowered at him, trying to decide whether he was being insolent or merely polite, but the other's prim features offered no clue.

'Well, don't stand there like a stuffed dummy!' he exploded. 'Shut the door.' And slumping into his chair he relit his cold pipe, puffing at it furiously.

Warburton approached, his nostrils twitching delicately at the clouds of stinging tobacco smoke.

'I presume, sir,' he said, 'that our friend Mr. Strange has been making his presence known to you?'

Crow glared at him beneath knitted brows.

'Who the hell told you?' he snapped. 'And anyway he's no friend of mine.'

'I employed the term in a merely rhetorical sense,' said the Sergeant, skipping the question the answer to which he thought was self-evident in the other's face. 'Though admittedly the activities of the person in question have frequently been of considerable value to us.'

'I'd sooner he kept his ruddy activities to himself,' snarled the other, 'and his prying nose out of jobs that don't concern him. Acting as if I'm not capable of making my own arrests without *his* blasted advice.'

The fumes from the evil-bubbling, battered-looking pipe seemed suddenly to overcome Sergeant Warburton, who was seized with a paroxysm of coughing.

'For Pete's sake stop that row!' rasped his superior unsympathetically, and puffed more furiously at his briar as he continued to rail against Jimmy Strange. 'This Zucci business — as if I can't pick up that slimy rat just when I want to.'

'Has the Strange individual suggested a method by which we could apprehend Zucci red-handed?' asked Sergeant Warburton and once again the other glared at him from beneath shaggy, suspiciously knitted brows. Was the Sergeant hinting at what both of them must know to be patently true: that hitherto Scotland Yard had never been able to pin a thing on Zucci, precisely because they'd never succeeded in catching him actually engaged in his notorious dope-running activities. And if Crow *could* nab him as a result of Jimmy Strange's tip, he would have cause to be damn grateful to that gentleman for supplying him with the first opportunity he'd so far had of settling Zucci's hash good and proper?

Once again, however, Warburton's aesthetic features beneath the Inspector's aggressive scrutiny were as free from guile as those of a babe newborn.

'There are moments,' Crow grunted, scratching his great cleft jaw pensively, 'when I'm not quite sure that you are as stupid as you look, Sergeant. That some of the footling things you drip aren't really meant to be smart at my expense . . . On second thoughts, though, I suppose you're so dumb you aren't even clever enough to be insubordinate!'

Sergeant Warburton, who didn't know whether he was expected to feel embarrassed or flattered by this backhanded compliment, blushed a delicate shade of pink and shifted from one foot to the other.

'And stop hopping about like a cat on hot bricks!' the other bellowed at him. 'Cripes! Here have I got a tricky job on and you all of a fidget — I can't ruddy well hear myself think!'

The Sergeant stood like a statue.

'Now then,' growled Inspector Crow, puffing grimly at his pipe, 'let's see about our midnight jaunt to this 'Black Lizard' place.' And hunched over his desk, he began setting in motion the detailed arrangements for their visit to the nightclub.

★ ★ ★

Meanwhile Jimmy Strange had returned to the 'Coronet' just as the last turn was reaching its finale.

'Enjoy your drink?' Sandra smiled at him, as he lounged into his seat beside her.

He nodded. Said nothing.

She regarded his profile. Apart from a certain tightness round the jaw and narrowness in the gaze which was directed towards the stage in purely perfunctory interest, it told her little. Enough, however, to warn her he was up to something. She watched him light a cigarette abstractedly and sighed.

He turned suddenly. With a quick warm grin took her hand in his. He said:

'All right, darling. One day I'll quit the racket and we'll have a cottage in the country with wistaria round the door and my slippers warming on the hearth.'

She said:

'And feel miserable as hell.'

He chuckled.

She said:

'Come to think of it, I'm not so crazy about wistaria anyway.'

He clicked his tongue in mock exasperation.

'There you go. I get you a place with wistaria, so you don't like wistaria. All right, we tear down the wistaria, what do you want now?'

She said:

'A drink. Large size.'

'You took the words out of my mouth. Let's beat it before the crowd starts.'

Outside as they got into a taxi, she said:

'Where are you taking me?'

'The 'Black Lizard', darling.'

She eyed him suspiciously.

'Sounds like a dump to me.'

'It is, darling.'

They drove off. A little while later:

'Hello, Zucci.'

The plump, bald man stared at him hard. ''Oo are you?' he muttered, in a thick, sibilant accent. 'I don't know you.'

'That's all right.' Jimmy smiled at him pleasantly. 'I know you.'

'Ees zat so?'

'Like a word in your ear.'

'I am a-listenin'. Shoot.'

Jimmy nodded towards the dance band that was beating out its jungle rhythm, stridently cacophonous. He said:

'Trifle noisy for — er — polite conversation.'

'I am not deaf.' The other, studiously disinterested, smoothed the lapel of his double-breasted dinner jacket with a pudgy hand.

Jimmy's eyes were suddenly icy, though a little smile continued to quirk the corners of his mouth. With calculated deliberation he drew at his cigarette and blew a cloud of smoke into the other's face. Through the smoke he murmured:

'Now, if it was just . . . shall we say, Harry Bell at the piano . . . we could talk here without having to shout.'

Zucci's expression didn't change, only the fat hand smoothing his lapel froze still.

''Arry Bell? 'Oo ees 'e?'

'No, you wouldn't remember him. He was only on the 'phone to you less than an hour ago.'

'Tell me more.'

'Just that he'll be round to see you soon.'

'Ees zat all you know?'

Jimmy nodded. Then added slowly: 'I forgot to mention, he knows you've double-crossed him, and if you don't pay up he'll squeal.'

The other was staring at him now, unblinkingly.

'What ees your name?'

He told him.

'Strange by name an' strange by nature, eh?'

'The quip *has* been cracked before.'

The pale snake-like eyes wandered across the small, half crowded dance floor — it was early yet, presently it would resemble a tin of sardines — to Sandra, whom Jimmy had left at a dimly lit corner table with a drink, telling her to relax and he'd be back in no time.

'Like her?' he smiled at Zucci. 'Little old-fashioned. Thinks this dump is run primarily as a nightclub.'

Zucci said:

'Per'aps the band ees leetle noisy. Come into the office.'

Zucci's office was up a short flight of stairs. It was luxuriously furnished, thick carpet, soft concealed lighting, massive, richly-carved desk; all the trappings. As the plump man closed the door, completely cutting out the dance music from the club, Jimmy noted the heavy curtains that masked what he knew were french windows leading to the fire escape.

The other poured drinks from thick, cut-glass decanters.

'One t'ing you say interes' me,' he said, as he handed Jimmy his drink.

'You surprise me,' Jimmy mocked him over the rim of his glass.

'You say 'Arry Bell know I 'ave double-cross heem and unless I pay up he will — 'ow did you put eet — squeal?'

'I did put it something like that.'

The other eyed him carefully. Then he turned his gaze to his drink and again that pudgy hahd was smoothing his coat lapel. He sipped and said softly; ''E daren't . . . '

'Shouldn't count on that,' Jimmy murmured. He chuckled inwardly and said through a puff of cigarette smoke: 'Anyway, I didn't come to the 'Black Lizard' to try your liquor, or to wise you up on something you know yourself.'

'So?'

'I happen to have a score to settle with Bell. It occurred to me we should cooperate maybe and — er — fix him between us.'

'Tonight?'

'No time like the present.'

There was a little silence.

Then Zucci said thoughtfully: 'I do not quite understan' 'ow 'e know I double-cross heem.'

Smiling thinly, Jimmy said:

'How do *I* know your bright idea was to clean him out of the stuff he was bringing over for you, and so save yourself the trouble of paying him?'

The hand on the lapel lay motionless.

'Tell me, I am mos' interested.'

'Because people are born with tongues in their faces. And you know what tongues do, Zucci? Wag. And if you were good at arithmetic at school, two and two make four. Me, I'm that smarter still, I can add up and make 'em *five*.'

'All right. So what about Bell?'

'Simple yet subtle. When he gets here to ask you a lot of leading questions, leave him to your boys again. Only this time plant some dope on him. Twelve o'clock prompt I'm down there,' he nodded at the curtains. 'In the alley with the car. You give me the tip-off, I pop in, collect our mutual buddy, dump him where he'll be picked up by the police pronto. He'll have to talk plenty to explain away what he's doing with the dope they find on him, Catch on?'

The other nodded slowly. 'Ees good idea.' He laughed. It was an unpleasant sound. There wasn't much amusement to it. 'Yes, 'e'll 'ave to talk much aplenty to wriggle out of *that* spot.' He spread his hands. 'An' anything 'e says about me ees only 'ees word against mine.'

'You catch on perfectly.'

Zucci's laugh filled the room as the plan caught his imagination, appealing to him more and more.

'Ee's great scheme! *Great!*' he guffawed.

Jimmy chuckled, too. Then he explained how the other was to signal him on the dot of midnight. As he listened and nodded agreement Zucci's great stomach fairly wobbled with mirthless laughter.

★　★　★

In the shadow of the fire escape, Inspector Crow breathed stertorously.

Behind him crouched Sergeant Warburton wearing an expression of repugnance, as the odour from a nearby dustbin drifted over to him. Pity, he was reflecting, that the Inspector wasn't smoking his pipe at this particular moment, the aroma from that blackened, bubbling bowl, foul as it was, was infinitely preferable to the one afflicting his senses now. Behind Warburton, three other hefty-looking policemen were tensed for action.

'Whassertime?' Crow whispered hoarsely.

'One half-minute to midnight, sir,' murmured the Sergeant precisely.

The other grunted.

'Soon's we hear Strange's whistle, up we go.'

'I have faithfully memorized the melody from the rendition hummed by you, sir, so that I shall recognize it at once,' Sergeant Warburton said pedantically.

'Then recognize it *now!*' rasped Crow, as the tune came to their ears, suddenly whistled from above. Clear and loud it came. 'Come on, dance to it!' barked the Inspector, pulling his bowler-hat more firmly on his bead, and starting up the iron stairs like some hippopotamus arising from the swamp. He cursed horribly as he slipped and missed his footing, but Sergeant Warburton gave him an energetic boost from behind and with an angry roar the lumbering figure charged on up.

★ ★ ★

Some time later Jimmy called Scotland Yard and got Crow, just back in his office. After a few minutes he replaced the receiver of Sandra's cream-coloured telephone and crossed to where she was snuggled in a deep chair. He was still chuckling to himself as he picked up his drink. Sandra glanced up at him quizzically.

'Is it so funny as that?'

'Zucci's expression, when Crow and his bunch busted in, instead of me, must've looked pretty comical!'

'And poor Harry Bell, how about him?'

'Poor Harry Bell nothing. Don't waste your tears on that flash dope-peddler, just because he could croon to rhyme 'June' with 'moon'.' He took a drink. 'Wonder what tune he'll sing to the judge?'

'He was caught then?'

'Bell, Zucci, plus the dope. The whole bag of tricks.'

'Mr. Crow must be very pleased with you.'

Jimmy grinned. 'You should have heard him at the other end of the 'phone.'

'You mean something went wrong?'

'I kidded him I'd be there at midnight to give him the signal for action.'

'But you've been with me since we left that 'Black Lizard' place around eleven.'

'Just what I explained to Crow.' He chuckled again. 'He sounded upset at missing me, and I told him I didn't know he cared. He started making horrible gurgling noises so I rang off.'

Sandra said:

'Didn't he get the signal?'

'Umm . . . ? Oh, yes, Zucci gave it all right. I told him what it was. Just whistle a little tune. Simple.'

And Jimmy whistled a snatch from one of the songs Harry Bell had sung.

6

The Body in the Callbox

It was a room, second floor back, in Soho.

If that conjures up in your imagination a narrow box, meanly furnished, its wallpaper that had once been a Surrealist's nightmare now — happily perhaps — shabby and faded, its floor bare but for a strip of cracked linoleum, then the picture you've formed in your mind isn't far out. Add a battered iron bedstead, a dirty washstand in the corner, couple of rickety chairs, a glaring electric light bulb suspended overhead and the scene's complete.

Not exactly the sort of room you'd wish on yourself for a long stay. Not that its occupants were habitually of the variety who stayed long in any room. They were transients. Ships that pass in the night. Here today and gone tomorrow. Could be this restlessness, amounting almost to a complex, on the part of many who rented this sort of room was merely the gratification of a repressed desire: on account of their long stretches spent in enclosed, barred spaces of narrow, restricted dimensions without being able to move on when they'd felt inclined.

As, for example, the present tenant of this second floor back, a character calling himself Louis Mayne. The smoke from his chain-smoked cigarettes had made the atmosphere so you could burn holes in it with a blowlamp. The fog was being added to by the cigarette drooping from the mouth-corner of a recent arrival, who wore a light-coloured snap-brim on the nape of his neck and sat astride one of the chairs. Louis sprawled on his bed, staring up at a peeling patch on the ceiling. He said:

'I tell you I'm goin' to get him if it's the last thing I do!'

The other leaned over the back of the chair pleadingly. But listen, what'd be the good? You'll only find yourself takin' the eight o'clock jump. And for what?'

'Because while I was rotting on the

Moor he took Lily away from me.'

'Aw, but Louis, there's as good fish in the sea as ever came out of it.'

'Maybe.' He spat out a bit of tobacco viciously. 'But I don't let anyone take from me what's mine. Give us another drink.' His companion got to his feet and removed his and the other's glass to the mantelpiece, which was adorned by a half-empty bottle of whisky and a soda-siphon.

'Well, I'm damned if I'd run my neck into a noose,' he said emphatically, as he mixed a drink and took it over, 'for some skirt.' And added: 'Who couldn't have been so sweet on you, anyway.'

Louis glared at him balefully.

'She did care,' he said through his teeth. 'Swore she'd wait till I got out. And then that smarming rat — ' He broke off to take a gulp from his glass. Then he said: 'An' don't be so sure I am taking such a helluva risk.'

'What d'you mean?'

For answer, Louis twisted round and lugged a revolver from under his pillow. It had a peculiarly long barrel. The other man stared at it, eyes bulging apprehensively.

'Where'd you get that?' he said hoarsely.

The answering grin was wolfish. 'Never you mind. See this?' He patted the curious-looking barrel. 'Silencer.' And pushed the revolver back under his head.

His companion shook his head. 'That won't help you. I tell you they'll get you for it.'

'I can take care of myself. But I'll get *him*, you can bet your shirt on that.'

He gulped off his drink and lay back, staring up again at the patch on the ceiling, his eyes malevolent slits, his thin lips a twisted bitter line.

★ ★ ★

Dusk was descending on Jermyn Street with the silence of a cat pouncing on a mouse as Jimmy Strange and Sandra came out of the 'Mirrobar' and turned down a side street towards the restaurant, where they had an appointment with a Lobster Thermidor. They walked quickly, for they were a little late, and the 'Mirrobar' cocktails had made them hungry, especially for Lobster Thermidor.

Jimmy was staring into Sandra's eyes, which were bright starry in the twilight, when the sharp sound of breaking glass made him bring up his head with a jerk. It had come from a few yards in front of them, and he caught a glimpse of a dark figure hurrying off and disappearing into the shadows.

'What was that?' Sandra asked.

Jimmy didn't answer. They were about to pass a callbox that stood on the kerb and he paused suddenly.

'Just a minute.' He turned to the telephone box and pulled open the door. As he stared down at the crumpled figure on the floor, he heard a voice, distorted and as if from far off, from the receiver, which was dangling at the end of its cord.

'Hello . . . ? Hello . . . ?'

With one movement he grabbed the receiver. It was a man speaking.

'Hello, who is it?'

It may have been only his imagination, coloured by the sight of the inert shape at his feet, but he thought the man sounded tense, anxious. Quickly he wrapped his handkerchief over the mouthpiece, muffling his voice.

'Hello?' he said.

'Is that you, Eddie?'

He hesitated a fraction. Then: 'Eddie speaking.'

'You sound a bit funny. What's wrong?'

'Sore throat.'

'Oh. Where you been?'

'I — er — was delayed.' He contrived to flash a reassuring look to Sandra, who, with an air of resigned bewilderment, waited a couple of yards away. He hoped she wouldn't decide to come and inquire more closely into what he'd meant by suddenly shooting off to the telephone like that. She wasn't used to seeing bodies lying around. The voice in his ear was saying;

'Well, anyway, I can't see you tonight . . . And listen . . . I got bad news for you, Eddie . . . Louis is out.'

'Louis?' Obviously the name was supposed to carry some special significance.

'Came back from the Moor yesterday,' the other went on. 'Remission of sentence.'

Jimmy said: 'So he's out?'

'Yes.' Then meaningfully: 'Thought you'd better know.'

'Er — thanks.' Adding: 'When are you meeting him again?'

'Got a game o' snooker with him tonight. The Greek Street Rooms.'

'I see . . . What time?'

The voice said after a moment's hesitation: 'About nine. But I'm telling you keep off the grass.'

'You're telling me,' was all Jimmy could think up in reply to that.

'Ring me tomorrow, see. Maybe we'll fix up something.'

'Sure.'

'Okay.' And he rang off.

Thoughtfully, Jimmy replaced the receiver. He paused to survey the body by the dim light of the callbox. In appearance the man was youngish, dark. Jimmy bent and expertly extracted a wallet from an inside pocket. It contained little of interest — except a name and address, obviously the dead

212

man's: Eddie Hill, Flat B, Soho Mansions . . .

Jimmy replaced the wallet and, his foot crushing two or three slivers of glass on the floor, stepped out. He glanced up and down the darkening little street. The distant rattle and hoot of a taxi in Jermyn Street, but no one in sight — except Sandra. Quickly he moved to her, ignored her questioning look, took her arm and walked a short distance, then stopped.

'Just what would this little pantomime be in aid of?' she asked, her tone excessively sweet.

He lit a cigarette. He said: 'Afraid, darling, you'll have to toy with that lobster on your little lonesome.'

'Charming,' she mocked him. 'But charming!'

'Listen,' he said, and she caught a grimness round his mouth that wasn't there before. 'Something slightly unfunny's happened. So be a nice baby and don't argue.'

'I suppose you couldn't tell me what's bothering you?'

He sighed. 'Such an inquisitive girl.'

'Coming from you, that's practically amusing.'

He said: 'There's a body in that callbox. It's extremely dead.'

She gave a little gasp of horror. 'But how — ?'

'Remember you asked me what that breaking glass was? Someone had shot him' — he nodded over his shoulder — 'while he was phoning. Used a silent revolver.'

She shivered. 'How horrible . . . '

He put his arm round her protectively and drew her close.

'Not nice,' he agreed. 'I'll have to find a cop. No need for you to be mixed up in it, so let's park you at the restaurant first.'

Their destination was only a few steps farther on. They reached it quickly. At the door she said:

'How long will you be, Jimmy?'

He shrugged non-committally. 'As long as it'll take to put a cop on the job. But you go ahead. Have a whacking great drink and forget what's happened.'

She eyed him steadily. She said:

'Which of us are you supposed to be

214

trying to kid, darling? You know darn well if I see you again tonight or even this week I'll be lucky.' She caught her breath in a little sigh. 'I wonder if this is how we'll look to each other when it gets to the last time I shall see you?'

'You know me, darling, the old bad penny every time.'

She nodded, her eyes still searching his face. 'But suppose,' she said, 'just suppose . . . one time when you turn up, I shouldn't happen to be waiting?'

He regarded her for a moment, his expression puzzled. He said: 'Suppose, just suppose . . . we cross that bridge when we come to it.' Then his seriousness vanished and he grinned. 'You go on in and get yourself on the right side of that drink. And keep one warm for me.' He was gone.

Only a stray cat shot out of a doorway as he retraced his steps swiftly, and a lonely taxi cruised past. He glanced into the telephone kiosk to reassure himself the body was still there, and continued on his way to the corner of Jermyn Street. On a corner diagonally opposite he spotted a policeman. He went across.

'Got a little job for you.'

The constable was a hefty individual with a genial expression. 'You have, sir? And what may that be?'

'Body in callbox down that street.'

'Dead, I presume?' was the matter-of-fact response.

Jimmy nodded.

'Oh, well, in that case perhaps I had better look into it,' said the other amiably, producing a handkerchief and carefully blowing his nose. 'Bit nippy for the time o' year, isn't it?' he observed conversationally as he accompanied Jimmy over to the other corner and down the narrow street.

As they went, Jimmy told him briefly how he'd heard the noise of breaking glass, noticed someone hurry off and had found the body. He avoided any reference to Sandra, or to his discovery of the dead man's identity.

'Was it a man or woman, sir, you saw running away?'

'Man.'

'No chance of identifying him if you saw him again?'

'No chance.'

'H'mmmmm . . . ' They reached the 'phone box and the policeman yanked the door open. He stood gazing down at the huddled figure with pursed lips. Pawing his chin reflectively, he turned to make the sententious comment: 'Looks dead all right . . . ' He broke off with an exclamation.

There was no one there.

'Blimey,' he said unnecessarily, 'the blighter's hopped it!' And in a tone of pained resentment: 'Without so much as a 'good evening' to remember him by.'

Which was the way of Jimmy Strange when occasion required it.

The taxi he had grabbed on emerging from the shadows, which had separated him from the cop and the callbox, drew up outside Soho Mansions and he got out. He surveyed the building with a speculative eye. It stood in a not particularly salubrious neighbourhood and was a smallish, shabby-looking block of flats. There were shops on one side, on the other a delicatessen and an all-night café, whose varied odours of cooking lay unappetizingly heavy on the evening air.

Jimmy found the entrance to the flats, the door of which was slightly open. He pushed, but the door stuck halfway, and he went into the ill-lit hall. There was no lift and he went quickly up the stone stairs. He located Flat B on the top floor. There was a long pause before the door opened in answer to his ring. The blonde who faced him was hard-faced, hard-eyed and hard-voiced. Without taking the cigarette from her mouth, she said:

'What is it?'

Jimmy had quite decided views on the subject of feminine pulchritude and this one, though she was pretty enough, didn't make much of an appeal to him. Too tough, and he didn't like 'em that way. Life was tricky enough as it was with guys handing out the tough business, without women acting that way. They should be so you could relax with them. He told himself he could relax with this little number as easily as with a boa-constrictor.

All the same, it wasn't like him to be ungenerous, so he gave her his warmest smile. 'Forgive me for troubling you,' he murmured, 'but this would be Mr. Eddie Hill's flat?'

'He isn't in, anyway.'

'I see . . . I wonder if I might talk to you a little — er — more privately?'

She stared at him, then down at his foot, which he'd unobtrusively placed inside the door. Her blue eyes as they met his again were like bits of very hard stone. He grinned at her disarmingly.

'All right,' she muttered.

As she closed the door and followed him into a small sitting room she seemed to soften somewhat. She said: 'I've been waiting for him. He's late. I wish he'd hurry.'

He thought he detected a note of agitation in her voice. He studied her with a long appraising look from beneath lowered eyelids. He calculated she didn't know Eddie was no longer of this world and he thought she probably hadn't had any hand in pushing him off into the next. From contemplation of her drooping lipstick-smudged cigarette, he looked round the room. He said:

'Nice little place he has here.'

She said:

'You a friend of Eddie's?'

'Sort of.'

She sat down, crossing her legs, automatically exhibiting them to their best advantage. He'd been thinking there was a suggestion of weariness about her and then his gaze travelled to her legs. They were definitely alluring and he enjoyed looking at them.

She caught his glance and her lip curved mockingly.

'Make yourself at home,' she said.

He smiled at her agreeably.

'I was thinking,' he said.

Which was perfectly true. She eyed him up and down through a puff of cigarette smoke. She said:

'What's your name?'

'Smith.'

She said slowly:

'One of the mysterious type, eh?'

'No, just careful.'

'What you got to be careful of?'

He was silent for a moment. He took a cigarette from his case, lit it, and exhaled abstractedly. He said, elaborately casual: 'Oh . . . quite a few things a chap should be careful of.' He paused, regarded the tip of his cigarette.

'Such as?'

He answered her almost reluctantly. 'Such as being shot in the back, for instance.'

There was a little pool of silence. Then her voice low and grating:

'What are you getting at?'

He looked at her.

'Does Eddie mean much to you?'

She stood up and faced him. 'What's happened to him? What's happened to Eddie — ?'

'I found him in a callbox off Jermyn Street.'

'Dead?'

He nodded. With a convulsive shudder she closed her eyes and swayed slightly. He watched her impassively. She might be putting on an act, he didn't know. If she was he had to admit she was doing a nice job. He said;

'Can you use a drink?'

She muttered something that he took

to be 'yes', and indicated a cupboard. He crossed to it with alacrity, produced a bottle of Scotch, syphon and glasses. He poured her a good shot and she took a long gulp. While he was mixing one for himself he suddenly wondered how Sandra would take it if ever anything happened to him.

The thought came to him smack out of the blue and he dismissed it as quickly. Must be growing morbid! He grinned to himself and glanced at his watch. Sandra would still be at the restaurant. He hoped she wasn't feeling too bad about him. He'd 'phone her soon as he got out of this place.

Over the rim of his glass he said to the girl:

'I suppose you wouldn't have any ideas about it?'

She answered him slowly, forcing the words out as if they tasted of the bitterness that consumed her.

'Louis did it. It was Louis.'

Jimmy said softly:

'The one who's just out of Dartmoor?'

She nodded: 'I heard tonight. I was

going to warn Eddie.'

He glanced at her interrogatively.

'Warn him?'

'I used to be Louis' girl.'

He knocked back his drink. So that's how it was. He'd walked into as cosy a setup of sordid passion and hate as maybe. With murder tacked on for good value. He thought depressingly how much more improving for his mind would have been the Lobster Thermidor — and Sandra. He sighed. Ah well, he was in it, might just as well get on with it and out of it, making it snappy all the way. He put down his empty glass and contemplated it regretfully.

She was saying:

'Where is Eddie?'

Almost absently he said:

'The police.'

She stood close to him.

'You're a dick, aren't you?'

He shrugged. 'I've been called all kinds of names.'

'You'll fix Louis for this, won't you?' she said fiercely. 'You'll fix the swine — '

She broke off suddenly and slumped into

a chair, stared at the floor with wide dazed eyes. 'Eddie! Eddie!' she moaned. 'I knew he'd get you! I knew he'd get you . . . '

He thought it was time for him to beat it. He felt a cynical repugnance for the way the whole damned box of tricks was working out. The idea of dog biting dog never did appeal to him. That the ruthlessness of the underworld was never more callously unleashed than when the crook revenged himself against one of his own fraternity he well knew. But it wasn't that so much — he was equally aware you didn't have to dig so deep to learn how savagely the law of the jungle prevailed. Just scratch society's upper crust, any place you chose, and you'd find it wasn't so far behind the underworld when it came to the claw-and-talon business. He knew, too, Eddie had probably asked for it, though that didn't square up with this Louis wiping him out. What really ate into him was the fact that a sordid story of jealousy and revenge, climaxing in murder, had been played around a tough little piece both men would have got sick to the stomach of sooner or later, anyway.

So Louis would get his, and within half a dozen Scotches after they'd given him his necktie the blonde would be fixing her makeup for the next guy.

He tapped the ash of his cigarette and said to her, his voice sharp-edged:

'Come on, take it easy. If it'll make you feel any better, the ex-boy-friend's got it coming to him, so everything will be cosy.'

A little later he slipped unobtrusively into the restaurant off Jermyn Street and sat down in front of Sandra. Her eyebrows were raised in surprised inquiry, her lovely mouth curved in an incredulous smile. She said:

'This *is* nice. Will you be staying long?'

He grinned back at her. He thought how good it was to look at her, how adorable she was. His heart felt lighter, and when the waiter put a large Scotch at his elbow it fairly floated on air. He said:

'Was going to 'phone you, matter of fact. Then remembered you might be missing me so thought I'd drop in.'

'Thanks for the memory. I presume

you called to say you've got to hurry on your busy way and to apologize — I hope — for ruining my evening. Correct me if I'm talking utter nonsense, won't you, darling?'

He took her hand.

'Sorry, precious, but that's how it is.'

'Oh well, it's heigh-ho for *another* early night. I'm told this asleep before midnight thing is wonderful for one's looks. Personally I can't quite get the idea of looking wonderful if no one's looking at you!'

'There should be a crafty answer to that,' he said, 'only it escapes me for the moment.'

'I know, darling,' she commiserated mockingly; 'it must be awfully difficult for you to think witty thoughts when your mind's all caught up with dead bodies in 'phone boxes and revolvers that don't go bang.'

He was regarding her intently. Then very earnestly he said:

'Come to think of it, that early-to-bed stuff's really got something. You are growing more lovely lately. Your hair, your eyes, your skin — there's a certain extra beauty about them that's been hitting me almost without realizing it.' He stared at her again in critical admiration, nodding his head in comprehension. 'That's what it is,' he murmured. 'Just sleep. Wonderful.' He drained his glass. 'Wonderful,' he said.

She patted an ostentatious little yawn.

'You must croon a lullaby over me sometime,' she said. 'Just now if you'll sing for a taxi it'll do.'

He saw her into a taxi and gave the driver the address, then turned and cut through a side street, down the Haymarket, heading for Whitehall. The subtle scent she used clung to him as he walked quickly. Automatically he dusted his shoulder with his handkerchief, a tender little smile playing round his mouth.

Just off Whitehall is a small hostelry known to its large and discriminating clientele as 'The Policeman's Lot'. A not inappropriate name for a pub but a tankard's throw from Scotland Yard, and which is frequented by officials during off-duty moments snatched from that respected institution in need of alcoholic solace or stimulation before repairing to their respective beats or other duties.

On occasion, too, 'The Policeman's Lot' was an agreeable rendezvous for gentlemen who ordinarily pursued lines of business not entirely compatible with that followed by the keepers of the law. It was not impossible to find a character notorious for his predilection for the theory and practical demonstration of safe-cracking rubbing shoulders with a detective-sergeant. In fact, the interesting spectacle might sometimes be witnessed of a gentleman newly released from a sojourn behind prison walls celebrating that event by a return of drinks with none other than the officer who had been directly responsible for his incarceration. Or an official might lend an ear to a whisper of information from a furtive mouth tipping him off about some projected nefarious activity, which, acted upon, would produce gratifying results — for the police — and a discreet reward for the informer.

Jimmy glanced at his watch as he

turned into 'The Policeman's Lot' and gazed round the crowded bar expectantly. The man he sought should be present. He sighted the familiar figure hunched over a corner table, a half-empty glass before him. His bowler hat was tilted off his furrowed dome, and his eyes, beneath shaggy ginger brows, held a faraway look. He might be deep in philosophic contemplation, or he might be merely thinking of his supper. Or again, he might be thinking of nothing at all.

Jimmy grinned and sat down beside him.

'I'll have a Scotch,' he said. 'Large.'

Inspector Crow jerked his head up with a start. He regarded Jimmy with an expression that was distinctly hostile.

'What the ruddy hell are you doing here?' he snarled.

'Having a drink with you.'

The Inspector's complexion went slightly mottled, then he drew a long shuddering breath. He turned to the man next to him, an aesthetic-looking individual, and grunted: 'Buy the — er — gentleman a drink.'

Sergeant Warburton's mouth compressed in prim protest, but he rose obediently.

'Bring me another beer,' Crow bawled after him, draining his glass with a noisy gulp and wiping a large hand across his mouth. To Jimmy he said heavily: 'So what?'

'So this,' said Jimmy, producing Eddie Hill's wallet.

The other glared at it suspiciously.

'It won't bite,' Jimmy reassured him. 'It's imitation crocodile.'

Crow shot him a dirty look, took it. Opened it. Face expressionless he said:

'Where'd you pick this up?'

'Where'd you think?'

'I'm asking the questions.'

Jimmy smiled amiably. Said: 'You must have been a beautiful baby, but most awfully spoilt.'

'All right,' growled the Inspector, with, for him, remarkable patience. 'Where-did-you-get-it?'

'Off the owner.'

Crow gave him a sidelong glance. 'Hill's dead,' he muttered

'Yours truly tripped over the body.'

'In the callbox.'

'Somebody's been telling you things,'

Jimmy mocked him.

'Why'd you disappear after tipping off the constable?'

'On account of I don't much care for cops. Except one,' he added with a sweet smile, expressly for the other's benefit.

'You haven't come here for me to take care of this,' the Inspector muttered. 'Or to tell me you like the colour of my eyes.'

'I don't,' said Jimmy emphatically. 'They're nasty little piggy eyes. Though I admit they suit you.'

Whatever horrific response Crow intended — and the veins round his neck swelled ominously — was interrupted by the return of Sergeant Warburton with the drinks. He handed Jimmy his, his nostrils a twitch with disapproval. Jimmy grinned at him affably, but the Sergeant turned his eyes away and sipped delicately at his lemonade

Over his drink Jimmy said to Crow: 'Here's to crime, flattie — '

The other swallowed half a glassful, choked and spluttered: 'Are you going to tell me what's your game?'

'Same as yours.'

'What are you driving at?'

Jimmy sighed patiently. He said:

'You want to pinch Louis Mayne, do you or don't you?'

'Louis Mayne?' Inspector Crow's eyebrows drew together in puzzlement.

'That is the person who came out of prison yesterday,' volunteered Sergeant Warburton, pedantically. 'Released before completing his full term, having obtained remission of sentence.'

'I know all about that,' Crow snapped at him. 'Get on with your ruddy lemonade!'

'Very good, sir,' said the Sergeant, blushing slightly.

The Inspector turned to Jimmy.

'What the hell's Louis Mayne got to do with Hill?'

'Nothing at all, except for the fact he rather neatly rubbed him out.'

'You seem damn sure Hill was murdered. Suppose it was suicide?'

Jimmy eyed him with affected surprise. 'Self-evident as it is that the amount of intelligence reposing beneath that repellent bowler of yours could be balanced on a pin, even you'll admit that committing suicide by shooting yourself in the back a shade far-fetched. Or,' he added agreeably, 'perhaps you'd like to try it for yourself some time? You might succeed.'

The Inspector was breathing heavily. He was not, however, in the privacy of his own office where he could, and frequently did, blow up as loudly as he liked. With a superhuman effort he controlled himself to speak relatively calmly to the object of his simmering rage.

'Suppose it is murder, I'm still asking you where Louis Mayne comes into it.'

'Know anything about love? No, you wouldn't. But there is such a thing knocking around. Even cheap crooks like Eddie Hill and Louis Mayne get tangled up in it. In this case Eddie pinched the other's girl while he was in clink. Not unnaturally Louis takes a poor view of this, in fact he rather dwells on it, he's got plenty of time to dwell on things where he is, so when he comes out — '

'He exacts his jealous revenge upon the man who had robbed him of his sweetheart,' put in Sergeant Warburton.

Jimmy grinned at him. 'You took the

very words out of my mouth.'

Crow scowled at the Sergeant and rubbed his great jaw reflectively.

'It adds up so far as it goes,' he admitted. 'But you bet your bottom dollar Louis will've fixed himself a nice little alibi. We'd have a hard job proving he even knew this Eddie Hill.'

'Could not the young woman involved be interrogated?' suggested the Sergeant.

'What the hell good would that do?' rasped the other. 'Some floozie's word against his, that's all.' He went on in aggrieved tones: 'I wish you'd shut your trap when I tell you; can't you see I'm thinking?'

Jimmy said:

'No need to go straining yourself. Better leave it to me.'

The Inspector eyed him sourly.

'What's your idea?'

'Louis will be playing snooker at the Greek Street Rooms around nine o'clock tonight — '

'How the hell d'you know?' the other began.

'Mind your own business,' Jimmy cut

in curtly, 'and try and concentrate on what I'm telling you now.' He lit a cigarette, blew out a long spiral of smoke and proceeded. 'We'll work to a simple formula. It's great charm is it's so simple even you can't make a mess of it.' He brushed aside Crow's angry growl and went on. 'All you have to do is march into this Greek Street place at the time mentioned, interrupt our friend's game and ask him politely to come clean about Eddie Hill. Louis will, of course, come the injured innocent and probably ask you to please repeat the name it's so unfamiliar to him.'

'Then?' grunted Inspector Crow.

'Then . . . you give him a quick look-over and find the evidence.'

'But what evidence?' queried Warburton sceptically. 'Surely you do not expect he will be carrying the revolver with which he perpetrated the alleged crime?'

'Why d'you rattle on as if you've just swallowed a ruddy dictionary?' Crow barked at him, and the Sergeant went back to his lemonade. The other peered at

Jimmy from beneath beetling brows. He said:

'*Is* that what we'll find on him — the gun he shot Hill with?'

Jimmy shook his head slowly.

'I imagine he's smart enough to have disposed of that, just in case. Though you'll be able to check where he got it — routine stuff.' He examined the tip of his cigarette pensively. 'No gun. But something else, and dear Louis won't be smart enough to talk himself clear of that.'

He stood up suddenly, knocking the Inspector's elbow so that the remains of his beer slopped over. Jimmy mollified his muttered protests.

'Sorry if I startled you out of your slumbers.' He licked his lips. 'My, my, how this chin-wagging dries up the larynx. I think a little throat-spray is indicated. What are you using, Gorgeous? More beer? And my winsome Sergeant Warburton? Come now, throw discretion to the winds and knock back another lemonade.'

And with an odd little glint of

amusement in his eyes, Jimmy made his way to the bar.

★　★　★

It was ten minutes past nine and in a shadowy corner of the smoke-hazed room a lean-faced man was scribbling a note.

Only one of the tables was in use and the sounds of the snooker game in progress together with the voices of the two players came to him as he folded the piece of paper and eased himself out of his seat.

Louis Mayne was saying as he vigorously chalked his cue:

'Hell, am I out of practice! Haven't even potted a red yet.'

His companion muttered commiserations and made his stroke. Louis watched, cigarette-end stuck to lower lip, his prison pallor accentuated by the greenish light over the table. The shot failed and he said perfunctorily:

'Bad luck.' He moved forward. 'Now let's show what I can do.'

He bent, then suddenly raised his cue

and glanced over his shoulder. 'Who was that just went out?' he frowned.

'Dunno. Why?'

Louis shrugged.

The other said: 'Noticed him when we came in, sitting there. Been waiting for someone who hasn't turned up, I expect . . . Good shot.'

'Not good enough,' Louis muttered, scowling. Then at his companion's startled exclamation, his head came round with a jerk.

'Strike a light, Louis! Cops — !'

'Take it easy,' he said, through the side of his mouth. 'They got nothin' on me.'

He eyed the approach of the new-comers with sneering indifference. The leading figure lumbered up to him, heavy jaw stuck out aggressively.

'Louis Mayne?' Inspector Crow rasped.

'What of it?'

'Want to talk to you about Eddie Hill.'

The hard eyes were expressionless. 'Who?'

'Hill. Eddie Hill.'

'Never heard of him.'

Crow said:

'In that case you wouldn't know he was found, earlier this evening, in a telephone box near Jermyn Street, shot dead?'

'You got big enough ears. You heard what I said.'

The Inspector's eyes glittered balefully. Came a delicate cough from Sergeant Warburton as with deliberate unconcern Louis began to chalk his cue.

'You needn't bother with that,' Crow said, 'Get your coat on.' He added over his shoulder: 'Give him a hand, Sergeant.'

'Very good, sir.'

Louis waited, smiling thinly, while Sergeant Warburton fetched his jacket from the peg. Slowly he rolled down his shirtsleeves, fixed his cuffs and then allowed the other to help him slip the coat on.

'Thanks!'

'Would you care for me to search him, sir?' asked Warburton primly,

'If His Lordship doesn't object,' the Inspector grated.

'Go right ahead,' Louis sneered. 'You won't find any gun on me, if that's what you're looking for.'

And then he was staring at the object the Sergeant had taken out of his pocket. With a grunt of incredulity Crow took a step forward, his hand simultaneously digging into his own pocket. It dug vainly and his mouth opened and closed like a great fish.

Warburton was saying with prim composure:

'A notecase, sir. Bearing the name, 'Eddie Hill', and address, '5, Soho Mansions' — '

By exertion of tremendous effort Inspector Crow managed to pull himself together sufficiently, at any rate, to grab that mocking rectangle of imitation crocodile. He shook it vigorously in Louis' face, whose eyes continued to bulge at it.

'So you'd never heard of him, eh?' he ground out between his teeth, contriving to cover up his own confused astonishment at the sight of the thing by bringing into play his full powers of vindicated accusation.

'I — I don't know where it came from — '

'No doubt Eddie made you a present of it when you weren't looking,' Crow snorted with heavy sarcasm. 'Just before you shot him in the back!'

'I tell you, I — ' Desperately the other tried to find words to talk his way out of the trap. But, as Jimmy Strange had prophesied, he couldn't make it. Like a cornered rat he could only gape at the wallet as if mesmerized. To him it meant the shadow of the gallows falling across him. His companion didn't help much either by leaning across the billiard-table and crying out wildly:

'I warned you not to, Louis — I warned you!'

'Shut up!' Louis snarled at him. Then tried to make a dive for it.

But Sergeant Warburton, anticipating the move, tripped him neatly and sent him sprawling full-length. As he lay, the breath knocked out of him, the bracelets snapped and the game was over.

As they prepared to move off, Inspector Crow suddenly bent with a grunt and picked up a folded slip of paper from the floor. He must have jerked it out of the

241

wallet when waving it at Louis. Unfolding it he read, his ginger eyebrows jutting forward in outraged bristles, his breathing growing stertorously apoplectic:

'*For Sourpuss with love.*'

7

The Vanishing Diamonds

Not least among the attributes and other possibly less commendable qualities that go to make up that forceful, unpredictable and somewhat elusive character of quixotic charm known as Jimmy Strange is a capacity for self-criticism.

In fact, Jimmy would go so far as to explain that he personally rates his happy possession of this ability habitually to check up on himself — sure antidote to the poison of self-deception — second only to his indisputable capacity for absorbing Scotch. Of which latter occupation he was not entirely without experience.

As he puts it with typical succinctness:

In the strata of high society where I dig, the chap who kids himself along might just as well go buy himself a wreath.

Which was why for some time past he had been viewing the situation between himself and Sandra with certain misgivings.

Guilty misgivings at that.

He hadn't been giving her a straight deal. He knew it and calculated she wasn't entirely without her suspicions either. One thing you didn't have to tell Jimmy Strange about: if there's anything concerning a woman of which you can be categorical, it's the certainty that her intuition will find you out — almost from the very flicker of an eyelid — when you look twice at someone else.

Women being, as has been observed before, funny that way.

Not that there was anyone else with Jimmy. No one in particular, anyway. But that he'd looked twice and then some more at this pretty face or that was something else again. It wasn't that he'd changed about Sandra either. She attracted him as much as ever. He felt the same way about her as he'd done right from that moment he'd first met her at the 'Rainbow'. He knew there was no one who could really take her place.

Probably, he reflected, that was where he'd gone wrong about her. Maybe he should have changed about her. He ought to have settled down by now into a nice steady warm affection for her, growing ever fonder. Instead of which she thrilled him more than any woman he'd ever known, and he didn't know what the world would be like without her. Except it would be hellishly grim.

None of this stopped him eyeing the next pretty piece he met in his speculative way and thinking along the lines of least resistance. Sometimes, regrettable as it is to record, he put his thoughts into action. Like that sultry brunette he'd met over the Brummel Snuffbox business. There'd been others. He wasn't any hypocrite so he knew he hoped they wouldn't be the last either.

Thus Jimmy Strange mused as he turned into Hatton Garden one bright sunny morning, and in a few moments found himself outside the firm of George Raphael. He had the notion some expensively attractive offering, while it wouldn't ease his own conscience, would give Sandra considerable pleasure and do something to persuade her she was the one he truly cared for. It would also postpone the inevitable showdown she was sooner or later bound to demand, and he'd like it to be later.

Old George Raphael was a personal friend of his and would certainly have something in the diamond line that should rate the sort of look he liked to see in Sandra's lovely eyes.

He went in and was received effusively. While the tubby, rosy-cheeked little man was bending his pince-nez over a tray of gems on the counter before them, the door opened and a tall individual wearing a dark Homburg came in. Raphael glanced up and greeted the newcomer deferentially.

'Oh, good morning, Mr. Carter.'

'Morning.' The other's manner was brisk and business-like. 'Those diamonds arrived from Westbourne?'

'Yes, sir, just come in by post. I haven't opened the package yet.'

'Like to see 'em.'

'Certainly.' He turned to Jimmy. 'I

won't be a moment, if you'll excuse me.'

Jimmy nodded and continued his inspection of the tray while Raphael hurried into his office just behind him. The sound of a package being unwrapped could be heard — and then a sudden silence. The next moment came an exclamation, then a gasping cry and the old man stumbled out, his face stricken. He was carrying a small cardboard box and part of the wrapping in an agitated hand.

'What's the matter?' snapped the man in the Homburg.

'The — the diamonds — !' choked Raphael, sagging against the counter and clutching it for support. 'They — they're not here — '

'Not there?'

'They've gone!'

'Gone?'

The diamond merchant dropped the box on the counter with a gesture of hopelessness and despair. 'Look!' he gasped. 'The diamonds — gone!'

The other grabbed the cardboard container and frowned at it. He shot a penetrating look at Jimmy, who'd moved nearer then stared again at the box. 'Good lord!' he exclaimed, pulling at the wrappings. 'What's this?'

'Bits of sugar,' gulped Raphael. 'Nothing but bits of sugar.'

Jimmy observed that was all in fact the box contained several pieces of sugar, of, he noticed, somewhat odd shape.

★　★　★

Sometime later Jimmy Strange was in company with other thirsty individuals helping to maintain the bar of 'Joe's Place' in Greek Street in its appropriate upright position by leaning against it. Deciding it would be more propitious to look in some other time about his prospective purchase, he had quitted Raphael's, leaving the distracted old chap telephoning Scotland Yard. The man called Carter had briskly taken charge of the situation, handing out advice in his business-like manner, and Jimmy had made an unobtrusive departure Not without, however, having assimilated some not unimportant aspects of the mystery of the vanished diamonds.

Sandra, whom he was meeting for lunch, was with her hairdresser, which gave him an hour or so's profitable drinking in hand before he collected her. He was turning over in his mind various points about the odd business at Raphael's, when a voice muttered in his ear:

'Hello, Mr. Strange.'

He turned from contemplation of his Scotch to regard the face of Frankie Willis. He murmured a reply, and correctly interpreting, without any effort at all, the other's expectant look, asked him to name his poison. Willis named it.

'Here's to crime!' he grinned, raising his drink. Followed a long pause, then smacking his lips Willis put down his glass.

'To say I needed that,' he said, 'would be what you might call an understatement.'

'Purely as a matter of academic interest,' Jimmy murmured, 'which of the two would you rather be without — that,' he indicated the other's drink, or good music?'

Willis, who was a cardsharper by profession with an incongruous fondness for classical concerts, considered the question for a moment. He shook his head.

'Difficult to answer. When I'm a-leaning back listening to music I reckon that counts most, when I'm a-leaning against a bar listening to this gurgling down then I reckon this takes the prize.'

Jimmy nodded sympathetically. 'I know how you feel,' he said. 'Myself, though, it wouldn't be a question of drink and *music*.'

Frankie Willis, who'd met Sandra, grinned slyly.

'Unless it was the music of a cutie's laughter,' he offered. 'The symphony of a curvaceous figure.!

'The things you think of,' Jimmy remarked. 'Change the record and jingle me up a Scotch.'

The barman brought the drinks. Over the rim of his glass the other said slowly:

'You been to Westbourne, I suppose?'

Without batting an eyelash Jimmy said casually: 'Sure.'

'Quite a nice dump. Fun and games. Very select and hoity-toity, but I like it that way.'

'So glad.'

Willis was regarding his fingernails with sudden elaborate interest. Without raising his eyes he observed:

'There's a smart jewellers down there.'

Jimmy glanced at his watch and said:

'I should be moving.'

He made no effort to move, but gave Frankie Willis a sidelong glance. The man said, still without looking at him and in the same tone of complete disinterest:

'Branch of Raphael's of Hatton Garden. The Westbourne shop's run by a chap called Kirot. Got a son, Paul Kirot.' He took a drink absently.

Jimmy produced his cigarette case, lit the cigarette the other took with a nod of thanks, then lit his own. He calculated Willis should unload what was on his mind any minute now.

Frankie Willis laughed through a puff of tobacco smoke. He said admiringly: 'You're a poker face, Anyone'd think I'm talking clean over your head.'

Jimmy said; 'So . . . what *are* you talking about?'

'The diamonds that did one of those vanishing tricks.'

'Tell me about it.'

'As if you didn't know.'

'As if I didn't know,' said Jimmy. Adding: 'Think I've got time for just a very small double.' And he gave the barman the same-again sign. As he took his, Willis said, keeping his voice only just loud enough:

'A little bird chirped me an earful just now. Didn't catch hold of the details. Not my line, precious stones. Always say they lead to *breaking* stones on the Moor.' He chuckled. Jimmy smiled at him pleasantly.

'You will have your little joke.'

Willis grinned, gulped from his glass and went on:

'Seems these diamonds got — er — lost in the post between Kirot's place and Hatton Garden. Anyway, when the package arrives at Raphael's this morning the sparklers are goners. The bloke who'd borrowed 'em had slipped some bits of sugar in their place. Perhaps he thought

252

they might sweeten old Raphael's temper when he finds the stones aren't there.'

Jimmy discreetly refrained from asking the other where he'd picked up such factual information, within a relatively short time, of the event's occurrence. From experience he knew the underworld was, in some mysterious manner, almost invariably aware of its members' contemplated operations long before they were put into execution. And the grapevine, that breathed the furtive whispers of what dark and secret machinations were in the air, reached out far and wide. Jimmy was satisfied to ask no questions and retain the confidence of his circle of acquaintances, which included useful informants — such as Frankie Willis among a number of other characters — who were usually calculated to be in the know. He said:

'All makes a jolly tale for tiny tots, but what makes you think I should be interested?'

'Well . . . I don't suppose your girlfriend would look sideways at a chip of ice' — he used the slang term — 'if you were to drop one into her pretty little palm.'

Jimmy said:

'Some ice can be very hot. I'd hate to burn her fingers.'

Willis shook his head emphatically.

'Don't get me wrong. I'm not suggesting you should cut in on the missing stuff. But suppose it was to find its way, safe and sound back to its rightful owner?'

'Go on supposing.'

'And *you* were responsible for their safe return, wouldn't old Raphael slip you a chip all for your ownsome out of gratitude? Get the idea?'

Jimmy, who'd already had the idea and been working on it the past hour or more, smiled at him affably. He said:

'Frankie, you have a lovely mind. I will duly ponder over your kind suggestion and maybe even act upon it.'

'Good,' Willis said heartily.

'Now I really must — '

'Just before you go,' the other interrupted him. 'Listen. Bend your ear closer.'

Jimmy regarded him with a quizzically raised eyebrow, then humoured him.

Willis put his mouth near and muttered:

'Charlie Mitchell is catching the two-thirty non-stop to Westbourne this afternoon. Staying at the 'Majestic'.'

Jimmy pulled thoughtfully at his cigarette and eyed him narrowly through a cloud of smoke. This was not uninteresting. Decidedly not uninteresting. Charles Mitchell was a 'fence' who dealt exclusively in precious stones. He chuckled admiringly at Frankie Willis. He certainly knew what went on. Glancing round the crowded bar, he nodded towards an attractive blonde who was with a couple of loud-suited men near by.

'You'll be telling me next that little party has a mole eight inches below her left shoulder,' he grinned.

Willis glanced at the blonde, who caught his look and flashed him a bright smile of recognition. He turned and said promptly:

'She hasn't.'

Then he joined in Jimmy's laughter.

★　★　★

As the two-thirty Westbourne Flyer drew out of London on its non-stop run to the coast, Jimmy Strange, from his comfortable seat in the refreshment-car, stared out of the window with a far-away gaze. He looked up out of his reverie only when the waiter came along to take his order for a large Scotch. Then sank back into his contemplation of the swiftly passing scenery until the drink arrived.

Sandra had remarked his preoccupation during lunch.

'What type of skulduggery is the Master Mind contemplating this time?' she asked sweetly. Too sweetly.

His explanation that he proposed making a trip down to Westbourne that afternoon didn't exactly draw coos of delight from her. She gave him a level look of speculation from beneath her raised eyebrows.

'Alone, of course?'

He nodded. 'Little job I want to take care of down there.'

'Blonde or brunette job?'

He grinned at her. He said:

'If I said, you wouldn't believe me.'

She said:

'Not a damned word. Still . . . it helps make conversation.'

'We could talk about the weather,' he said. 'Or even you.'

She said:

'Or even us.'

The *maitre d'hôtel* had interrupted them to inquire anxiously about the chicken soufflé, which had, he volubly declared, been specially prepared for them under his own watchful eye. On being reassured by Sandra that the dish was delicious he drifted away, leaving Jimmy adroitly to steer the conversation away from the theme that her last observation had dangerously directed it.

Now, as he took a drink, he told himself he had no greater incentive, anyway, for pulling off the Westbourne business successfully. For he felt it would take nothing less than a nice slice of ice to ease his relationship with Sandra along the way he wanted it to go. With no strings to it and no breakup either. A little smile quirked the corners of his mouth as he recalled the simple philosophizing of

Frankie Willis on the subject.

He drew an early edition of the evening paper from his pocket. They'd given the Vanishing Diamond story front-page headlines and plenty of space. Not that it told him anything he didn't know. Or couldn't have added a few details to.

In fact the report was given over mostly to descriptions of the Hatton Garden premises, the firm of George Raphael's long-established association with the diamond business, plus a photograph of the old boy, which Jimmy reckoned must have been taken by the first camera ever invented. There was a lot of stuff about the package arriving apparently un-tampered with and the discovery of the pieces of sugar in place of the precious stones. There was a statement from Kirot of the Westbourne branch he personally had packed the diamonds for dispatch, and the police seemed satisfied the theft must have occurred some time in transit. The gems, seven in number, were extremely valuable.

Jimmy raised his eyebrows at the figure quoted in the paper. Not a bad haul, he mused, and turned to the Stop Press. It carried a brief paragraph, which gave precisely no further news about the mystery and ended with the traditional bromide about the police being actively engaged upon investigations and expected to issue an important statement shortly.

One vital fact about the case had passed unnoticed, Jimmy observed, not without satisfaction. Smiling broadly to himself, he pushed the newssheet aside. He lit a cigarette, leaned back, allowed his thoughts to drift now on the business ahead of him, now on the lovely slenderness of Sandra's legs, and the train rushed on towards Westbourne.

★ ★ ★

Jimmy surveyed himself critically in the mirror, gave his black tie a touch so that it butterflied with infinite exactness above his impeccable evening shirt. With a silver-backed brush he carefully smoothed a recalcitrant wedge of hair into place and slipped into his double-breasted dinner jacket. He glanced at his wristwatch. Time enough for a couple of drinks before dinner. In a few moments he stepped out of the lift and crossed the thronged foyer, automatically receiving and returning with equal interest the glances of two attractive brunettes and one ravishing blonde who stared at him as he went by.

He went into the cocktail bar and then paused momentarily as he caught sight of a little red-headed figure perched alone in a corner. Almost simultaneously she saw him, and with an excited squeak of surprised delight darted across and had twined her arms around his neck.

'Jimmee! Jimmee — '

'Gaby — !'

Which was about all he could manage to say before being smothered by her fond embrace and torrent of endearments, uttered in fantastic broken English mixed up with a flow of non-stop French.

'Ah, cher Jimmee! Quelle surprise! C'est merveilleuse! Mon amoureux! Ah, mon beau Jimmee — je suis trés exciter . . . '

And so on.

At length he finally contrived to

extricate himself.

'Well, well!' he gasped, chuckling a trifle breathlessly. 'You certainly don't pull your punches!'

'Oh, am I so glad to see you once more!'

'That's rather the idea I get.'

She laughed throatily and was about to fling herself upon him again, but he quickly took her arm and manoeuvred her towards the bar.

'I need something to brace me up after that attack,' he grinned at her.

He ordered drinks while the barman looked at him gravely, trying to conceal his amusement. Gaby was clinging to him, chattering full speed ahead. Her conversation, though sparkling with a vocabulary that was most fascinating to the ear, was somewhat difficult to follow owing to her habit of mingling atrocious English with breathtakingly rapid French. Whether she was herself conscious of the effect this amazing mixture produced on her listeners and deliberately cultivated her fantastic rigmarole was debatable. Jimmy, habitually sceptical of everything and everybody as a matter of principle, was privately of the opinion that Gaby was shrewd enough to know what was an asset and made use of it accordingly.

Her throaty chuckle and vivid accent wasn't her only asset either. Not by any means. And Jimmy, as he listened to her excited quick-fire chatter, was, if not all ears, certainly all eyes. She was a delicious piece of Parisian femininity plus.

He'd first met her some little time ago when he'd been backstage, for no good reason at all, at the 'Mayfair Casino', that song-supper-and-show place where the food's always cold, the wine warm but the girls, though by the amount of clothing they wear ought to be cold, are, as it happens, not.

Jimmy at that time had been losing interest in a little number who was chronically cuddlesome and, at the same time, as calculating as a cash register. He'd been standing in the wings watching Gaby going through her routine while pondering ways and means of sliding out of the aforementioned baby's life for ever and longer than that, when in the dimness that followed Gaby's act she'd bumped into him as she was hurrying off the stage. From then on they'd got along like a row of houses on fire with a timber yard thrown in.

The barman was placing their drinks before them and as he took the money he gave a discreet cough.

'Er — pardon me, sir,' he said to Jimmy hesitatingly, 'but — er — that is — '

Jimmy glanced at him.

'What's on your mind?'

'It's what's on your face, sir — if I may say so,' said the bartender gravely. 'The lady's lipstick.'

'*Ah, mon pauvre chérie!*' Gaby cried, leaping up and squeaking with laughter. 'Eet ees all over you.' She snatched his handkerchief and began briskly to rub his face. 'Your ear, your chin, your nose — I must poleesh heem off.'

'Thanks,' muttered Jimmy.

'*Voila,*' she laughed, pushing his handkerchief back into his pocket and pausing to survey him. 'Now you are all washed up!'

'I know what you mean,' he grinned.

He indicated a more secluded corner. 'Let's park over there and I'll let you tell me more about myself.'

'*Oui, chérie.*'

Over his shoulder he called:

'Bring a couple more in a minute.'

'Certainly, sir.'

Gaby sat very close to him and held his hand.

None of your inhibitions about her. As she'd once explained to him, in her own delightfully unique way, she'd lost all that sort of worrisome nonsense on the occasion of her debut at the *Folies Bergère*, at the same time that the solitary article of clothing she was wearing — she happened to be rather overdressed in a small rose — fell off just as she began her dignified descent in the grand staircase scene.

She thought Jimmy was extremely attractive and made no attempt to disguise the fact. Which was all very straightforward and refreshing and he enjoyed it. Always when he met her he asked himself why he didn't see her more often. Her allure was decidedly original, with her throaty accent, her comic English and her irrepressible vivacity.

He supposed the reason he didn't tag along more closely was because he'd caught that look in her eyes now and again that warned him she could go for him in a serious way and would, being Gaby, want him to reciprocate accordingly and more so. Which was something he didn't wish to get mixed up in at all. He liked her the way she was, but to get seriously involved would spoil the fun.

He returned the warm pressure of her hand and said:

'This is all very cosy. But what the devil are you doing down here? Aren't you in the Casino show?'

'Ah, you are not very *au fait* with my movements.'

He ignored the rebuke in her tone by deliberately misunderstanding her.

'I've seen you dance,' he said.

She squeaked with amusement. '*Non, non*. Eet ees what I am doing, I mean. Not any more at the Casino, I am rehearsaling the new cabaret at the 'Regis'. I am in this place to give a show for the *grande* Charity Ball tonight is being holding.'

'I must look in on it. You'll be giving the customers that veil dance, no doubt?'

She nodded vigorously.

'Why else they would ask me to appearance?'

'Why else, indeed. I mustn't miss a word of that.'

'Eet ees *tres artistique*.'

He smiled at her.

'I think you've got something there,' he said. And went on: 'What time d'you do your stuff?'

'Not until *minuit*.'

'So what are we doing till then?' he asked. 'Hungry? We could go in and eat to start with.'

'I am so sorry, chérie,' she pouted. 'But I cannot. I am already fix-up.'

'Too bad.'

She was glancing round the bar, 'He should be here *dans un moment*.'

'Would he be someone I know?'

She shrugged. 'Paul Kirot.'

He didn't make the slightest sign of a pause with the glass he was raising. Just drank a trifle thoughtfully, perhaps.

He said:

'Would he be the son of Kirot the jeweller by any possible chance?'

She nodded, eyeing him quizzically.

He said slowly:

'Is that so?'

'*Pourquoi?*'

'*Pourquoi* what?'

'You say 'ees zat so' in funny peculiar ways.'

He said:

'Pretty little ears you have and they don't miss a thing either.'

'They are missing your answer to my question,' she came back promptly. 'And there ees little look in your eyes which says to me the answer would be some intriguing.'

He chuckled.

'It goes like this . . . ' he began, then broke off as the barman put a couple more drinks before them. When he'd gone he said: 'Where were we?'

'Still here,' she said. 'And you were going to tell me a leetle story.'

'Not such a funny one at that. A

London diamond firm has a branch here run by Kirot. Some time back they send a fortune in sparklers to Kirot, on account of he thought he could do a deal with 'em down here. As the deal doesn't jell, however, they're returned. But when the packet's opened at the London end what do they find?'

'*Je ne suis pas.*'

'Less than that,' he grinned at her. 'No diamonds. Just some bits of sugar.'

'*Dieu!*'

'Kirot is emphatic the stones were packed all right, did the job himself. Cops, flatties, police, *gendarmerie* — do I make myself clear?'

'Clear as needle in mudpack!'

'They're certain the theft didn't happen in the post. Diamonds don't arrive. So what have you got?'

'No sparklingers,' Gaby said.

'No sparklingers. Correct. And why? Because, my delicious piece of nonsense, they were never posted at all.'

'Tell me that over again, please.'

'They were never — ' he began, but she interrupted him.

'Non, non! The delicious piece of nonsensicals part. I like the way you tell *heem.*'

'Gaby, this is no place to look at me like that. Concentrate on diamonds.'

'I do sometimes,' she smiled. Then nodded thoughtfully. 'What you say ees quite interesting. I must ask Paul about eet.'

'You friendly with him?'

She didn't answer at once.

He said:

'You can tell me. I'm not too young to know.'

'We are meeting either in London or 1 am down here sometime.'

'He must be using up quite a slice of pocket money.'

'He ees very generous,' she agreed. And added; *'Pourquoi pas?'*

'As you say, why not.'

A momentary frown crossed her face. She said:

'Lately eet ees the *chemin-de-fer* also he spend on. Gambling party nearly every night at a villa by the beach.'

He raised an eyebrow, then said: 'Me,

I'd rather hold your hand than a hand of cards any time.'

She flashed him a tender smile. With a little shrug she said: 'He ees going there tonight I think — ' She broke off and glanced over his shoulder. 'Ah! Here Paul ees now.'

He turned as two men came into the bar. 'The dark character?'

She nodded. 'I do not know who ees the other.'

He could have told her. It was Charlie Mitchell. They hadn't spotted Gaby, and he said quickly; 'Listen, Gaby — find out when your boyfriend's buddy goes back to London. Tonight. Tomorrow, when.' He stood up and grinned at her. ' 'Phone me soon's you know. I'll stick around till you do.'

'You are very mysterious.'

'Don't let it bother you. So long.'

'*Au revoir*, Jimmee. I telephone you.'

He gave her a mock conspiratorial wink and was gone.

A couple of hours later found him in a secluded corner of the hotel vestibule, listening idly to the dance orchestra dispensing from the restaurant a pleasurably sentimental accompaniment to some quiet drinking he was putting in. He was in a mellow frame of mind, though back of it a little dagger of uneasiness stabbed at him now and again. That was when his thoughts went around Sandra. He'd 'phoned her, but no reply. He wondered who she was with. He couldn't blame her for being with someone; all the same he'd have felt that much happier if he'd found her waiting for him to ring. He'd have liked to have heard her voice.

He'd told Reception he was expecting a call and where they'd find him. Now he looked up as a page hurried over and said:

'You're wanted on the 'phone, sir.'

'Who would be doing the wanting?'

His answer was the one he'd expected. 'Miss Fontan, sir.' The kid gave him a cheeky grin. He flipped him a coin and, wishing he didn't wish it was Sandra calling, went to the telephone-box.

'Where you talking from, Gaby?'

'From the 'Lighthouse Tavern', *chérie*.' It was an old smuggling inn, modernized

271

and with a clientele of the smart crowd. She was saying: 'Paul and his friend are in the bar, they not know I am telephone.'

'Smart girl.'

She giggled throatily. 'I feel like a crime novel! The other man's name eet ees Mitchell. And I can tell you thees, Jimmee, he go back to London tonight on the train who ees a quarter to one of the clock thees morning.'

The 12.45 that night, Jimmy translated, a sudden glint in his eyes. 'Thanks for the tip.'

She said: 'I not know why you so interested in heem. I not like thees quiet men who are looking hard always. He has got some business deal on with Paul, but who I not know.'

Jimmy smiled grimly to himself.

'Tell you all about it sometime.'

'I think you can think of other thing to talk of more amusing for me, *non*?' And went on cajolingly: 'You will be at my show tonight? Eef your *petite* Gaby not beeg enough attracting you, thees man ees there also with Paul before he go to train.'

'He hopes,' murmured Jimmy.

'Pardon?'

'Just a thought I had.' He went on easily, his concentration already fastening round the scheme he was evolving: 'Shall have eyes only for you.'

'And afterwards?' she insinuated.

'Depends on Paul.'

'Oh, he ees bring me back, then off gambling. He say he has much to win back tonight. Beeg fool I say, but eet ees wasting my breathing to speak So I am all on my loneliness in that great large hotel.'

'I'll be around, I shouldn't wonder.'

'You will come up to my suite for a night-hat?'

'Which is an idea, too.'

He rang off and made his way back to his corner, his expression somewhat preoccupied. The waiter brought him another drink; he relaxed and lit a cigarette. Yes . . . he thought, the pieces of the jigsaw were falling cosily into place. The way he saw it the completed picture looked something like this:

First, Paul Kirot had pinched the sparklers.

No doubt his father had packed 'em all right. But the son had got hold of the package before it was mailed and it would have been a simple job for him to substitute the sugar lumps in place of the original contents.

Motive for the theft: that good old-timer, young man tries to play the playboy without having enough cash to carry the role. Paul Kirot was playing around with toys like Gaby Fontan. Dolls in that class were an expensive hobby. Like a fool, the chap had tried to get hold of more cash by gambling. He'd plunged deep and now was floundering in as sticky a morass as maybe.

The diamonds due for return to Hatton Garden had given him a bright idea and he'd grabbed at 'em like a drowning man at the old

Young Kirot wanted a market where he could dispose of the stuff, and in fact had undoubtedly made his contact before he actually swiped the stones.

Which brought that dear character Charlie Mitchell into the picture.

Plain enough the 'fence' was down at

Westbourne on business. And from what Gaby had just tipped him it was evident the deal was being fixed that night. Which added up to something else: One, that Mitchell, who'd be present with Paul Kirot at Gaby's performance before catching his train, would be carrying the diamonds on him. Two, young Kirot, who'd ideas of recouping his losses by playing the gaming-table after the show, would have on him the cash he'd received from Mitchell.

Which, Jimmy concluded, was a situation offering possibilities that, to say the least, were interesting. He drew thoughtfully at his cigarette and turned those possibilities over in his mind.

Westbourne was definitely a smart town. Nothing of the popular seaside resort, with a summer influx of visitors followed by a dreary winter of inactivity and deserted boredom, about it. For its increasing prosperity the town relied on its popularity with Londoners of the well-to-do, sophisticated type who rented weekend villas all the year round and took their vacations there.

Westbourne prided itself on its 'Continental' atmosphere, which it assiduously cultivated. Its shops and cafés, cinemas and theatres wore gay and attractive exteriors, designed to cheer the eye. Pride of the town's architectural achievements was undoubtedly the Ambassador Rooms, a large building that could be used as a concert hall for the regularly visiting orchestras and artists and so on, while also making a magnificent ballroom.

Tonight the Ambassador was certainly jam-packed all night. No doubt the charity in aid of which the ball was being held was a most deserving one. All the same, it is a matter of speculation as to whether the crowds had that in mind very much, or whether Gaby Fontan was the magnet. Jimmy Strange, as he pushed his way through the throngs that were crowding in on the dance floor eagerly uttering her name on every side, smiled to himself. There was no doubt that the Fontan figure pulled 'em in.

It was close on midnight. Gaby was due to make her appearance on the miniature stage in a few minutes. Jimmy's gaze travelled to the couple of individuals he sought and his eyes narrowed as he drew nearer to them. They were standing right by the stage. The lights were dimming and the orchestra started to play the introductory music. The audience quieted expectantly and the curtain rose. Two spotlights threw dazzling pools of light centre stage, and in a moment Gaby stepped into their radiance, smiling at the rapturous applause that greeted her.

She began her celebrated dance.

From his position, which was now directly behind Messrs. Kirot and Mitchell, Jimmy watched her appreciatively. He'd seen her show several times, but it was the sort of thing only the most blasé wouldn't enjoy plenty times more. When it came to looking on while a seductive little redhead neatly began losing one after another of the half-dozen veils that were her only apparel to music, Jimmy wasn't all that blasé. Besides, he liked the music.

As the climax of the act approached he drew closer to watch. He knew precisely what would happen as that last veil flew off. The moment arrived. Gaby made a dexterous movement and — the spotlights went out. Stage and audience were completely blacked-out. Then the lights came on again, and as the applause crashed, drowning the music, Gaby was in the centre of the stage, a magnificent gown thrown around her, all smiles and bows.

To Kirot — she'd caught sight of him next to his companion — she flashed a special smile, covering up the pout of disappointment at her failure to see another figure who'd promised to be there.

But Jimmy had taken the opportunity before the lights came up again to slip away.

Back in his room at the Hotel Majestic he put a call through to Sandra. He rang for a long time, but either she was sleeping remarkably soundly or she was still out. Somewhat morosely, he figured she hadn't come in, and replaced the receiver. He lit a cigarette and drew a small wash-leather sack from his inside pocket and placed beside it a wad of notes. Cursorily he flipped through them. Mitchell had struck a characteristically mean bargain. He estimated the price he'd paid was only a fifth of what the stuff was worth. He tipped the bag and the diamonds sparkled and shone in his hand like live things. He eyed them disinterestedly through a cloud of cigarette-smoke, then replaced them and locked the wash-leather sack and the wad of notes away.

That little lot would make old Crow's eyes bulge when he popped them on his desk at Scotland Yard tomorrow. And he gave a little grin at the thought. The grin faded as his thoughts swung back to Sandra. Had he gone to all this trouble to earn a nice slice of ice especially for her, just for empty air? Not even her voice over the 'phone? He shoved the question aside. Let it wait, he'd get around to the solution to that in the morning.

Then the telephone jangled and, a smile quirking the corners of his mouth, he answered it. What the hell had he been worrying about!

'Hello, darling,' he said.

And the voice in his ear said:

'What about that night-hat, my naughty leetle Jimmee?'

He managed to cover up, make it sound as if he had meant the 'darling' for her. He replaced the receiver, stared at it for a moment, then with a shrug went out.

★   ★   ★

Gaby was laughing deliciously:

'Oh, I would give a meellion to look at the face of that foolish Paul when he finds hees money is disappearanced — and that ugly Mitchell creature, too, when *he* finds for hees diamonds!'

Jimmy, who'd merely given her a very sketchy account of what had happened, nodded across the rim of his glass.

Gaby went on:

'But what made you suspecting Paul in the start?'

'Remember the sugar? That gave me the idea from the kick-off the stuff had been pinched this end and by someone who visited this hotel. Then I bump into you, which is nice for two reasons, the second one being that you spill it about Kirot. I knew he hadn't been exactly avoiding this hotel because you stayed here, so it was easy.'

'I not comprehending what the sugar has to do with eet?'

'You take it in your tea and coffee?'

'*Mais oui.*'

'Then you've noticed it's not in cubes, but in flat oblong pieces.'

Vigorous nod of that lovely red head.

'But, of course. *A la continental.*'

'You've hit it. And the only place I know in this country where they serve sugar that way is — '

'The Hotel Magnificent, Westingbournes?' she queried.

'The Hotel Magnificent, Westing-whatever-you-say-it-is.'

She was regarding him with eyes wide and sparkling with admiration.

'But such a very clevaire Jimmee! *Merveilleuse! Merveilleuse!*'

'Glad you're impressed,' he grinned.

There was only the width of his glass between them as she said:

'Now one other leetle question you are telling me.'

'Being which?'

'Being which is how did you get back the sparklingers from Mitchell and also the cash from Paul?'

He smiled at her gently over his drink.

'That's part of my story over which I'd prefer to draw one of your veils,' he said.

And should anyone wish to know more of what happened afterwards — with regard, that is, to Jimmy's reward as anticipated from a gratefully generous George Raphael; and if Sandra received her present of a 'nice slice of ice'; and if she did what transpired as a result of the handsome gift, well, that's another adventure of Jimmy Strange.

THE END

DR. MORELLE MEETS MURDER
A CASE FOR DR. MORELLE
DR. MORELLE'S CASEBOOK
DR. MORELLE INVESTIGATES
DR. MORELLE INTERVENES
SEND FOR DR. MORELLE
DR. MORELLE ELUCIDATES
DR. MORELLE MARCHES ON
MEET JIMMY STRANGE

We do hope that you have enjoyed reading this large print book.

Did you know that all of our titles are available for purchase?

We publish a wide range of high quality large print books including:

Romances, Mysteries, Classics
General Fiction
Non Fiction and Westerns

Special interest titles available in large print are:

The Little Oxford Dictionary
Music Book, Song Book
Hymn Book, Service Book

Also available from us courtesy of Oxford University Press:

Young Readers' Dictionary
(large print edition)
Young Readers' Thesaurus
(large print edition)

For further information or a free brochure, please contact us at:

Ulverscroft Large Print Books Ltd.,
The Green, Bradgate Road, Anstey,
Leicester, LE7 7FU, England.
Tel: (00 44) 0116 236 4325
Fax: (00 44) 0116 234 0205

S.T.A.R. FLIGHT

E. C. Tubb

The Kaltich invaders are cruelly prolonging their Earthmen serfs' lives and denying them the secret of instantaneous space travel, so desperately needed by a barbaric, overpopulated Earth. While the Kaltichs strip Earth of its riches, the Secret Terran Armed Resistance movement, STAR, opposes them — but it's only their agent, Martin Preston, who can possibly steal the aliens' secrets. If he fails, billions of people will starve — with no place to go to except to their graves.

THE SILENT WORLD

John Russell Fearn

Around the world there was total silence from Pole to Pole. Seas crashed noiselessly on rocky shores, hurricanes shrieked mutely across the China Sea. People shouted and were not heard; alarms and bells rang and yet were mute. The dead wall of silence was everywhere — the most strident sound was unable to break through it. Scientists were unprepared for The Silence. There was something amiss with the laws which governed sound — but that was only the beginning . . .

DOUBLE ILLUSION

Philip E. High

Earth — four hundred years from now — a rotten society in which mankind is doomed to die out — and one seemingly average man with incredible I.Q. potential . . . An ultra-intelligent computer is built and used to govern humanity — and all corruption in the world is eradicated. Mother Machine decides what's best for her human children — and it is done. But the all-powerful computer is turning mankind into zombies. The world's only hope lies in one outlawed, not-so-average man . . .

A WOMAN TO DIE FOR

Steve Hayes

When hard-nosed PI Mitch Holliday loses his licence, he helps his partner, Lionel Banks, to pick up a missing girl named Lila Hendricks. But everything goes wrong; Mitch is drawn into a world of money, murder and double-cross. Seduced by socialite Claire Dixon's wealth — murder is now the name of the game. The target is a wealthy businessman with few redeeming qualities. Would Mitch, tough and cynical as he is, kill for the promise of love and money?

MEET JIMMY STRANGE

Ernest Dudley

Jimmy Strange was a mysterious young man who'd turn up when he was least expected; wherever there was trouble, he'd appear from behind some dark corner. No one knew much about him, though he was always a gentleman. He was never short of money, but where it came from no one knew. He wasn't a crook — yet they did say he could break into a house with the best of them — but always in a good cause . . .